The Grave Blogger

I0534534

Donna D. Fontenot

Published by DDtect Publishing

ASIN: 0615655572

DEDICATION

For McKayla and Donovan, with love, that they may know it's always possible to make a dream come true. Believe in yourselves as much as I will always believe in you.

ACKNOWLEDGMENTS

Many people helped me get this book written, some in inspiration only, others in more tangible ways. All were important to the process, and it would be impossible to name them all, but some that must be mentioned include:

Minnie and Percy Fontenot for being the kind of parents who taught me to believe in myself, to work hard, to take learning seriously, and most of all – they taught me how to love.

Sandie Thibodeaux and Gary Fontenot for being the best siblings in the world, and for always being there when I needed them.

My 3 StAmigas: Brigitte Daigle Caston, Gloria Silvia Thudium, and Lisa Fournet Saia for being insanely amazing lifelong friends.

My entire Facebook crew consisting of friends and family. They endured months of my writing process and suffered through endless snippets of the book as it was written. They were there to encourage and inspire.

My awesome Indiegogo contributors, Sandie Thibodeaux, Marcia Thompson Baldwin and Eric Wu.

Chapter 1

"Home Invasion Turns Deadly"

"Woman Missing, Presumed Dead, As Severed Hand Left Behind"

"Freezer Sold at Auction Contains Dead Body"

"Strawberry Fields Mask Several Graves"

"Case Mimics Deadly Jazz Club Shootout"

"New Orleans Killer Says It's Just His Latest Hobby"

"Bag Of Bones Reopens Old Shrimper Case"

"Two Decades Later, Bayou Family Slaughter Remains A Mystery"

Raya's mornings often began this way. As a freelance blogger working in the true crime niche, she spent most mornings researching cold cases. First, she'd run through an index of newspaper headlines extracted from various true crime websites. The first step was always based on hunches. If the headline caught her attention, she would copy and paste the headline, excerpt, and website address into her research folder for later perusal.

This morning shouldn't have been any different. More headlines, more hunches, and more copying and pasting than Raya liked to do. The drudgery of the mundane tasks of copying and pasting just drove her crazy sometimes, but she hadn't yet found a technological way to avoid that task. This morning was different though. Just as she'd pasted that last headline into today's document, she hesitated. Something in her gut caused a reaction unlike anything she could remember. Actually, that's not true. This reaction was just like something she'd felt before. It was a visceral déjà vu that went deeper than the normal feeling of having experienced something before. This was an emotion, a disturbance, a fear.

This morning was definitely different. "Two Decades Later, Bayou Family Slaughter Remains A Mystery" bounced around Raya's skull like a rubber ball.

The rubber ball turned into a voice ricocheting through her brain. "Do you think she understands what happened? Should we ask her what she saw? You already spoke to her?! Without me here? How could you do that! Well, of course she clammed up. She doesn't know you and she's just gone through the most horrific, unimaginable nightmare. No, don't lecture me and do not tell me to shut up! No!"

Raya's head snapped up and the voice disappeared.

"What the hell?" she said aloud, looking around her small apartment, half-expecting to find someone else in the room, though that of course would have been ridiculous. No one had ever been inside Raya's apartment. Well, at least not since the movers had brought in the few boxes and meager pieces of furniture 5 months ago.

Shaking her head as though that would actually clear her mind, she rose and went into the tiny bathroom, turned on the water at the sink, and splashed her face. "That works in the movies, but dammit, all it got me was wet."

Looking into the mirror, Raya studied her face as she had so many times before. Most people felt at home with their faces. Of course, nearly everyone found fault with their appearance, but despite that, each one recognized themselves in an innate way. No one felt out of place within their own skin the way Raya did. Every time she saw her reflection, she wondered who was staring back at her. The shoulder length dark hair, dark brown eyes, and latte-colored skin accentuated prominent but lovely cheekbones, a strong straight nose, and lips that looked as though they'd just had a treatment of Botox. Raya's face had an ethnic beauty that most women longed for, but the beauty meant nothing to her. It was merely a mask that someone had placed over her soul. For as long as Raya could remember, she'd never felt comfortable with herself, and never really felt as though she knew who she was.

She knew how to use such obscurity to her advantage, however, in both her cold case investigations and when hiding from virtual enemies in any of the online games she played obsessively. Having grown up in the age of the Internet with its abundance of online chat rooms and games, Raya understood the importance of masking her identity. Her anime avatar and fantasy-inspired username projected a strong image, providing her with a slight psychological edge over the gamers she competed against. Every gamer had his or her own strengths and weaknesses. Raya's strength was her ability to predict most of her opponents' next moves. To prevent them from carrying out those moves, Raya liked to use the cunning strategy of distraction, followed by a surprise attack.

This was the first time she'd ever surprised herself. The voices in her head felt like an unexpected attack that she'd launched against her mind.

"Ok, chickadee, why the hell did you go nuts just now? And why did that feel so freaking real?"

Taking a slow, deep breath, Raya returned to her desk and typed in the web address for the story entitled, "Two Decades Later, Bayou Family Slaughter Remains A Mystery".

Chapter 2

Two Decades Later, Bayou Family Slaughter Remains A Mystery

20 years ago, the little village of St. Felicity, just west of New Orleans, was rocked by the brutal murders of four people, all members of one of the town's founding families. Reporters at the time dubbed this crime the "Bayou Family Slaughter". In a scene reminiscent of a horror flick, authorities discovered Mayor Randy Broussard, his wife Alicia, their 14-year-old son Desi, and 10-year-old daughter, Grace, brutally murdered in their home.

When asked about the investigation, former Sheriff Gene Dupont said, "I'll never forget the shock of realizing what that family went through that night. The mind games that the killer played on Randy and Alicia just left me speechless. I've never seen anything like it, and I still hurt to think about the choices they had to make."

The choices Mr. Dupont referred to involve a cruel game that the killer apparently forced the family to play that night. Detailed "game instructions" were found at the crime scene which painted a very clear picture of the twisted events that played out that night.

Twelve posters, numbered sequentially, were taped to the walls of the home's adjoining living room and dining room, in what some later described as being reminiscent of the Stations of the Cross. Each poster had instructions printed using old-fashioned stenciling. The instructions for each involved two game aspects: that of chance and that of strategy. Each "station" required either one or both parents to choose between one of two options. Both choices involved pain to some member of the family, but if the parents failed to make a choice, a third more brutal attack would be carried out by the killer.

The four family members were found bloodied, tortured, and dead, sitting around the dining room table. The blood-spattered floor and walls at each poster "station" told the tale in vivid detail.

Despite years of effort, the killer has never been found, and the little village of St. Felicity wonders, 20 years later, if a madman still lives and works among them.

Chapter 3

The cursor on Raya's laptop screen was jumping crazily. Raya looked at her finger, resting on the laptop's mouse pad, and realized that her shaking hand was causing the cursor to dance out of control. Just as Raya often looked at the mask in the mirror, she now watched her physical reaction to reading the news story as though she were observing a stranger's reactions. Outside of herself, she could see the trembling hands, feel the chill of the skin, and watch her skin turn a pale ash gray. Nothing about this day was normal, and nothing would be normal ever again.

Raya picked up her cell phone and dialed.

"Mom? Can you come over? It's really important."

"Raya? You sound strange. You want me to come to your house? Are you okay? What's the matter, honey?"

"I'm okay, Mom. Sorta. But please, please, come over right now if you can. I need you."

"I'll be there in five minutes! Do I need to call anyone? Are you sick? Do you need an ambulance? Anything?"

"No, Mom, just you. I just need you. Please come now."

"On my way. I'll be right there."

Raya pressed the End button on her smart phone, dropped it on the desktop, and sat numbly, waiting. Flashes of both sound and images careened through her senses, threatening to overwhelm her with the intensity. Raya fought back, willing her mind to shut out the noise and squeeze the images smaller and smaller until they were just a pinpoint of animation. Four minutes later, the door banged against the wall, startling Raya, as her mother ran to her side.

"Raya, tell me what's wrong! What's the matter?"

Raya wrapped herself within her mother's arms, finally letting the tears burst out. "Oh mom, I don't know. I don't know. It's all so strange. I'm so scared. It's crazy. Maybe I'm crazy, I don't know. Mom, things are happening. I'm hearing things, seeing things, remembering things. Or, maybe not remembering. Maybe I'm hallucinating. Mom, what's wrong with me?"

"Honey, calm down, shh, calm down. It's okay baby, I'm right here. You're not crazy. You know you're the rock of this family. If you're crazy, then the whole world has gone mad, right? Right? There you go, shh. It's ok. It's ok. Momma's got you now."

Raya's mother, Janet, held her close, rocking her back and forth, continuing her calm assurances that everything was going to be fine. After several minutes, Raya's sobs quieted, and she was able to catch her breath and speak.

"Mom, like I said, I don't know what's going on, but I just read about something that happened in St. Felicity 20 years ago, and I swear, it's like suddenly I was there. I could see stuff - bad stuff, Mom - and it felt as though I was actually there. Mom, was I ever in St. Felicity when I was about 5 years old?"

"Oh my God. Oh Raya. We didn't think you'd ever remember any of it, I swear. I worried for so long, so very long. Oh God, it's finally coming back to haunt us - you. Oh, my baby, my sweet baby."

"Mom! What are you talking about? You didn't think I'd ever remember what? What happened to me back then? Why am I hearing and seeing all these crazy, horrible things? What do I have to do with the Bayou Family Slaughter?"

"Raya, honey, I think we should get your dad here too, and Dr. Forester. I promise we'll answer your questions, but I can't do this alone. Before I call them, I need to ask you a very important question though."

"What, Mom?"

"Raya, have you told anyone anything about this, besides me? Does anyone know that you are having memories of that time?"

"No, Mom, this just happened. I called you right away. Why?"

"Are you sure? This is very important, baby. Think hard. You didn't tell anyone else?"

"No Mom, I told you. This just happened. I called you right away and haven't spoken to anyone else. Well…except for the voices in my head."

"Ok, good, good. All right, I'm going to call Dad and Dr. Forester. I'll just be in the other room. Yell if you need me, ok?"

"Sure Mom, ok, No problem. Just hurry, all right?"

"I will baby, I will."

Janet stepped into the kitchen to get a little privacy and dialed her husband's phone. "Dennis, I'm at Raya's. Oh God, Dennis, she's remembering. Yes, yes, I'm sure. She's asking questions. Hurry over Dennis and stop by Dr. Forester's office and pick him up too. I'll call him and let him know you're on your way."

Hanging up, she immediately dialed another number. "Dr. Forester? This is Janet Landry. It's happened. Dennis is on his way to pick you up now. I didn't even think to ask if you could come now or not, but oh please, try. Oh good, thank you. Thank you."

Janet took a deep breath and walked back into the living room. "Raya, I just got off the phone with Dad and Dr. Forester. They'll be here in just a few minutes."

Chapter 4

Twenty minutes later, Raya's father, Dennis and a psychiatrist named Dr. Forester were bustled into Raya's apartment by Janet. Dennis gathered Raya into his arms, hugging her with the strength of a man who loves his daughter. When he finally let go, Dr. Forester grasped Raya's hand and introduced himself.

"Hello, Raya. My name is Dr. Jon Forester. I knew you when you were just a little girl. Do you remember me?"

Raya glanced at her parents, then back at Dr. Forester. "No, Dr. Forester, I'm sorry, I don't remember ever meeting you before."

"That's understandable, Raya. Most people retain very few memories of their early childhood. In fact, some memories aren't memories at all, but are simply the brain's way of latching on to stories parents tell, or photographs that document a moment in time. We often think we remember that time we made a snowman that we see in the photograph, but in reality, we are only remembering the photograph itself."

"That's true for me, I suppose. I really don't remember much about my childhood. But today..."

Gesturing towards the couch, Dr. Forester said, "Why don't we all sit down. Your parents brought me here because they know you've experienced something traumatic today, and they believe I can help. Of course, you're an adult, so it's up to you if you'd like me to stay and help or not."

Glancing again at her parents, Raya nodded. "Yes, yes, that would be fine, sure."

"Raya, can you tell us what happened today that upset you?"

"Yes, though honestly, I'm not sure any of it makes any sense. But I'll try to explain. I was going through headlines like always..." she said.

Dr. Forester interrupted Raya, saying, "I'm sorry, Raya. I'm not sure what you mean when you say 'going through headlines'. Can you explain?"

"Oh yes, sorry, I forgot that you don't know what I do for a living. I'm a freelance blogger. I have several clients who all run true crime websites. Every day, I look through old cases that have been documented on the Internet, going through all of the newspaper headlines that reference them. I copy and paste the headlines that seem the most promising - well, I guess promising isn't the best way to describe a murder, so let's use the word 'interesting' instead.

Anyway, I gather a few of the most interesting news headlines that I can find that day, so that I can start researching each one. If the research proves that the case would hold reader interest, I'll add it to my to-do file. Eventually, all the cases in my to-do file will be further researched and turned into a series of blog posts for the true crime websites that I write for."

"I see. Ok, so today, like any other day, you were going through the headlines. What happened then?"

"I saw one that just made me queasy inside. Now, let me tell you, I read about and write about a lot of really gory cases, so one little headline never has that kind of effect on me. I'm numb to it all by now. And really, the headline itself was pretty tame."

"What was the headline?" he asked.

"It said something like, 'Two Decades Later, The Bayou Family Slaughter Is Still A Mystery'", she answered.

Dr. Forester looked at both Janet and Dennis. The three of them exchanged looks that told Raya they all knew something about the Bayou Family Slaughter case.

"You know something. Every one of you knows something about this. What aren't you telling me?" Raya's voice climbed an octave, and her eyes danced wildly.

Dennis clasped his hands together. "Baby girl, it's okay, it's okay. We're here to tell you everything you need to know, really, honey. Calm down for just a minute, Raya. I promise you we'll answer all your questions. Okay?"

Janet reached over, grasped Raya's hand, and said, "We're here, baby. There's a lot to discuss, but please, let Dr. Forester help us get it all sorted, okay?"

Raya saw the love and concern in her parents' faces, and she thought she saw something else there as well. Fear. Raya could not recall ever seeing either of her parents showing the slightest bit of fear before, and she didn't want to see it now. Taking a deep breath, she said, "Sure, okay Mom and Dad. Yes. I'm sorry, I'll be patient. Dr. Forester, what else would you like to know?"

"Just continue on with what happened after you saw the headline and felt queasy."

"I don't know if you've ever fainted before, but I have - once. Just before you faint, it feels like the world around you is shrinking to just a pinprick of light. Remember those old Loony Tune cartoons where Porky the Pig would end each show with 'Th-th-that's all folks!'? When that happened, everything on the screen would fade to black except a circle around Porky, and the circle grew smaller and smaller, while the black screen got bigger and bigger. Know what I mean?"

"Yes, I remember that."

"Well, that's what fainting feels like to me, and that's the same kind of feeling I got today, only I didn't actually faint. Everything spiraled down to just a pinprick of light, and then someone was talking. It was like a voice inside my head, having a conversation with someone else. Only, I couldn't hear the other person speaking. It was like a one-sided conversation, similar to hearing someone speaking on a phone call."

Raya paused, and then continued. "So, this voice had a conversation, and she...it was a woman...she was asking someone if they should find out what someone saw. And then she got upset when the other person apparently told her they'd already asked that. The woman was mad that the other person had spoken to ... whoever ... without asking her permission first. I'm not actually positive that's what the conversation was about, but that's the impression I got. I don't remember the exact words now."

Dr. Forester leaned back and thought for a moment. "Raya, did you recognize the voice?"

Raya's head whipped backwards in surprise. "Recognize? I don't know. I'm not sure it was even a real person. I thought maybe I was just hallucinating. Wait, do you think it was real? Like a memory? Is that what you're saying?"

"I'm not saying that, no. At this point, I can't know for sure what you experienced. But if it was a memory, then perhaps you might know whose voice you were remembering."

"I see. I don't know. It was a woman's voice, like I said. It almost sounded like Mom's, but I don't know. I'm really not sure, right now."

"That's fine; you don't have to be sure. What happened next?" he asked.

"Well, the voice went away, and everything came back into focus, you know, like I was back in reality again. I shook it off and decided I needed to research that headline right away, to see if I could figure out why it had spooked me so much."

"So, you did research it, then?"

"Yes, briefly. I clicked on the headline and read the article. It gave a few details of a murder that happened 20 years ago in St. Felicity. That's a little town near New Orleans. Anyway, the more I read it, the more panicky I got. By the time I'd finished reading, I was shaking like crazy; I was cold, but sweating at the same time, and I was just feeling really scared. It was like I suddenly remembered everything I was reading, and yet...I didn't really remember any of it. I know; it's bizarre. It doesn't make any sense. I can't remember something and not remember it all at the same time. But I swear that's what it feels like! Anyway, that's when I called Mom and begged her to hurry over. And you know the rest. Now, would someone please tell me what's going on? Was I involved in that case somehow? Am I really remembering something about it? Or am I just losing my mind for no reason?"

Dr. Forester patted Raya's arm. "Raya, you're not losing your mind. You are experiencing some memories of a time in your childhood, and those memories are tied to the case you researched. It's a long story, and we've always wondered if this day would ever come. If you hadn't stumbled across that headline, maybe it wouldn't have. But you did, and here we are. Dennis, Janet, I do think we need to deal with this right now, but I'd also recommend that we all take it slowly. Raya, it's important that memories be allowed to resurface naturally when possible, rather than forcing them, so if it's all right with everyone, I'd like to guide us all through the story in a slow, measured way. Are we all agreed that I'll lead us through the past events then?"

Janet and Dennis both nodded, and it was clear that both were on the verge of panic themselves. This made Raya more frightened than anything she'd experienced today. She wondered to herself, if her parents were this afraid, just what would this trek through the past reveal?

Chapter 5

Dr. Forester concentrated for a few moments before speaking. "Raya, when you were 5 years old, you and your family lived in St. Felicity. In fact, you were born there, and lived there until the Bayou Family Slaughter murder took place. That night...the night that the police discovered the bodies...the sheriff called me to the scene. He and I were old friends, and I'd worked with the department on cases before. Sheriff Dupont gave me a very brief rundown over the phone of what had taken place and informed me that a little girl might have been a witness to the crime. He wasn't sure because she wasn't speaking or answering any questions. He hoped I might be able to get through to her."

"And I was that little girl?" Raya asked.

"Yes."

"But how is that possible? How could I have lived all this time—20 years! —without remembering that? I mean, even if I didn't actually witness the crime, surely, I'd remember the police, and you, and all the questions. This doesn't make any sense."

Raya's mother knelt on the floor in front of Raya, taking both hands into her own. "I know it doesn't make sense, Raya. But we've been told that the brain does strange things when it needs to protect us from things that are just too much for us to handle. Right, Doc?"

"That's true, Janet. Raya, you protected yourself from the emotional pain you experienced that day, and it's possible you would never have remembered anything—consciously—if you hadn't run across that headline. But now that you have, it's very likely that the memories will begin to flood back in, and you'll need to be prepared to deal with them. It's better that the people who understand the situation, and care about you, be here with you when those memories resurface. It's possible that the next few hours will bring it all back. We're here to help you deal with that if it happens."

"Okay, I'm sorry. It's just so strange", she said.

"No need to apologize. Now, are you ready to move on or would you like to take a break?"

"No break, Doctor. Let's move on. I need to know."

Dr. Forester continued telling the story of that night.

"After hanging up the phone, I drove over to Mayor Broussard's house. Once I arrived, Sheriff Dupont led me briefly through the crime scene so that I would have a better understanding of what happened there. Not that anyone could ever really "understand" such a scene, but nevertheless, I spent a few moments taking it all in. Next, he brought me outside and led me to the garage where he said they were keeping the young girl they'd found on the premises. He didn't know who she was or why she was there, but he hoped I could help clear up those questions as well.

When I walked into the garage, I saw the girl - you - sitting hunched over on the floor in the farthest corner. The garage was mostly empty. The mayor didn't keep cars in the garage. He mostly just used it for storing gardening equipment and the like. There wasn't anything large enough in there for you to hide behind, so it seemed that you were doing your best to just curl up and disappear into the corner of the wall. My heart went out to you at that moment, and I've cared about you ever since."

"Wait." Raya stood. "Wait, I have dreams about being curled up in the corner of a big room. They never meant much to me, except for the fact that I have them on a recurring basis. I always thought that was a little odd, but nothing more."

"I'm not surprised. You probably have other memories that manifest themselves in various ways. Some may be in dreams, but some may even be habits or quirks that are in your everyday life. In fact, your very career might be one such manifestation of those memories."

"So, did I open up to you? Did you find out anything from me? Was I a witness? Did I know what happened?" Raya sat back down, hoping to calm her nerves.

"You didn't speak to me at all that night. You never spoke a word to anyone that night, not even your mother and father, once we found out who they—and you— were."

Raya asked, "But if I didn't speak, how did you find out who I was and who my parents were?"

Raya's father said, "We heard about the murders at the Broussard home, honey, and we knew you were there. We panicked of course and called the police immediately to find out if you were okay. You were spending the weekend there. We'd just dropped you off that day. Mayor Broussard was your uncle - my brother. Your mom and I planned to go house-hunting, and when I mentioned it to your aunt and uncle earlier that week, they offered to have you stay with them for a few days, so we wouldn't have to drag you all around. They had such a nice place. We all thought you'd have fun. So, as soon as we heard that there'd been some sort of violence there—we didn't yet know exactly what— we called to check on you. We were far enough away that it would take us a couple of hours to get back, so calling was the quickest way to get information. Once we spoke to a deputy, everyone was pretty sure that the little girl who wouldn't speak was probably you. When we finally got there, Dr. Forester filled us in on what he knew so far."

"Mom, when you got there, did you ask Dr. Forester—or the sheriff, maybe—if you thought I should be questioned?"

"I did, honey, yes. I asked Dr. Forester, and he said he'd already tried to question you. I got pretty upset with him, I remember. Once I calmed down, though, I realized that he'd been as gentle as possible with you, and I was grateful to have him there."

"Okay, well, that explains that strange conversation in my head today then. That was you I heard. I don't know why I didn't hear both sides of the conversation though," Raya said.

"I can probably clear that up," Dr. Forester said. "Your mom was naturally upset, so her voice was raised, but I was trying to calm her down, so I was speaking very softly. We were standing about 20 feet away from you at the time, so I imagine it was fairly easy to hear Janet's voice, but not mine."

"All right, but I'm dying to know. Did I see what happened? Please, somebody tell me," Raya pleaded.

"Yes, Raya, as far as I was able to determine, you did witness at least some of what happened that day. However, none of us know exactly how much you saw, nor do we know if you actually witnessed the person responsible for the crimes."

Janet shifted uncomfortably. "Honey, there's something else we don't know, and it's the reason I asked you earlier if you'd spoken to anyone else about what you experienced today." She closed her eyes, hesitating.

"What, Mom? What don't you know?" Raya asked.

"We don't know if the killer knows you were there," Janet said.

No one spoke. Raya sat quietly, her mind whirling. Finally, she said, "So, it's possible that this maniac might want to find me and make sure I never have the chance to tell what I saw?"

"That's possible, Raya," her father said. "That's why we moved. That's why—well—that's also why we changed all our names."

The past 20 years that Raya had spent looking at the mask in the mirror all made sense now. She'd never been able to recognize herself because she wasn't the person she'd known herself to be. She wasn't Raya. The person in the mirror had another name at one time.

"My name isn't Raya? Did we change our last name? Is it not Landry? Wait, of course, it wouldn't be. You said Mayor Broussard was your brother, so that would mean your last name would have been Broussard too. Right?"

"Yes. That's true. I wasn't born Dennis Landry, and your mother's birth name wasn't Janet. And we didn't name you Raya."

"What's my real name, Daddy?"

"When you were born, we named you Maria. Maria Angelique Broussard. When we changed our names, we chose Raya for you because we thought it was close enough to "Maria" for you to be able to adjust. We'd often called you 'Ria' when we were playing with you, so Raya wasn't a big stretch for you to make."

"Maria. Maria Broussard. Would y'all mind if I take a few minutes to think this through?" Raya asked.

Dr. Forester said, "I think that's a good idea. Let's all take a break."

Raya rose, walked into her bedroom, and closed the door. Stepping in front of her dresser, she gazed at her reflection in the mirror. The face that stared back at her looked the same as always, but it showed a mixture of fear and peace that might have made little sense to anyone else, but it made perfect sense to Raya. Maria was looking back at Raya, and the mask no longer existed. The face in the mirror had reason to show fear, but it also had plenty of reason to reflect a kind of peace. The peace of finally knowing who she was made all the difference.

Raya walked back into the living room and announced, "Break time's over, folks. Let's get this story rolling. I want to know everything, and I want to know it right now."

Chapter 6

Janet and Dennis exchanged looks with Dr. Forester, who took a moment to consider his words carefully before he spoke.

"Raya, I wish there was a lot more to tell. Unfortunately, what we already discussed is just about 99% of everything there is to know. Or, at least, we've told you nearly everything we have knowledge about."

"Surely, there's a lot more to the story, Doctor."

"Certainly, there must be, but we aren't in that loop. It's likely the police know much more of the story, but we haven't been apprised of that information," Dr. Forester said.

"Ok, fine, then at least fill me in on the other 1% that you do know. When did we move? When did we change our names? Why didn't you try to get information out of me?"

Dennis said, "I can answer at least some of those questions. Remember I mentioned that your mom and I had gone out of town that weekend to look at houses?"

Raya nodded.

"I was in the process of going solo and starting my own consulting firm. St. Felicity was much too small a town to enable me to expand my clientele, so we were looking at various cities nearby. I'd already considered New Orleans and Baton Rouge, but Ethan Breaux, a business acquaintance of mine, suggested I check out an area with a lot of potential clientele, here in Lafayette. He said the need was just as great here, but the competition hadn't yet sucked the market dry. Anyway, that's why it took so long for us to get back to you, once we heard what happened. Since we were planning on moving anyway, it just made sense to do it sooner rather than later."

Janet interrupted her husband by laying her hand on his arm. "What your daddy is trying to say, honey, is that we felt we needed to get you away to protect you. We weren't offered the chance to go into Witness Protection because no one knew for sure if you had even been a witness to the crime. So, we took it upon ourselves to provide our own meager sort of witness protection. We went on an extended 'leave of absence', or so everyone we knew thought. We led them to believe we just needed to get away, to grieve for the family members we lost that day. In reality, we spent that time getting all our affairs in order, including changing our names. Once we returned to St. Felicity, we simply told our friends and neighbors that we'd decided to move to New Orleans. Then we moved to Lafayette instead. We never returned to St. Felicity, and we never spoke to anyone there again."

Raya looked puzzled. "But where do you fit into all this, Doctor? Obviously, you've spoken to Mom and Dad since then, or you wouldn't be here now."

"That's true, Raya. Actually, I moved here to Lafayette at the same time as you and your parents. We all decided that someone needed to be around in case your memory of that day returned. Obviously, they could have taken you to a new doctor here in Lafayette, but that would mean sharing your identity and none of us believed that was the safe thing to do."

"Well, Doctor, that's really generous of you to move just for me, but isn't that a little far-fetched? Since when does a doctor move his entire practice just for the sake of one patient? That's a little difficult for me to believe."

Dr. Forester smiled at her quick insight. "Your skepticism is warranted, I'll grant you that," he said. "Your parents and I discussed the situation at length. Let's face it. My practice was not going to grow much in a tiny village like St. Felicity. I was ready to move on, anyway, so it seemed like the right thing to do. I don't regret the decision at all."

The conversation stopped, as each waited for someone else to speak. Raya's mind struggled to handle all of the input of the last several hours. After several tense minutes, she finally broke the silence.

"Have there ever been any leads on who might have done this? Did the police even try to catch the killer? Are we just supposed to live in fear and secrecy for the rest of our lives?"

Dennis said, "I've kept up with the case as much as possible over the years. As far as I've been able to determine, there's never been much progress made in determining who was behind the deaths of your Uncle Randy and his family. Oddly enough, the killer left behind a lot of evidence, but none of it seemed to yield any real clues as to his identity. Of course, after a few years, the case took a back seat to other more recent crimes, as cold cases usually do. I do think the police did all they could at the time, but nothing seemed to pan out."

"I guess my memory loss didn't help much either, did it?" Raya said.

"Raya, even if you'd been able to tell everything you knew—if indeed you knew anything at all—it's probable that it wouldn't have helped much. You were only 5 years old. Adults rarely remember crimes they witness with any degree of accuracy, so the prospect of catching a killer based on a description from a young child's eyewitness account is extremely unlikely. Don't allow yourself to feel guilt over something that is out of your control," Dr. Forester said.

He continued, "Now that we've shared what we know about the events from that time, I'd like to talk about what you feel right now. You called your mother because you felt a strong connection to the story, and your brain unlocked at least a partial memory when you heard the conversation in your head between your mother and me. With all of this new information, has there been any change? Has the connection gotten stronger? Have any new memories surfaced?"

"Actually, no. I'm calmer now, even though I should probably be more upset now that I know that I was involved in all of this craziness. But I don't feel any more or any less connected to the events now than I did before you got here. And I definitely haven't remembered anything else. Maybe that means I really didn't see what happened?"

The hopeful look on Raya's face wouldn't stay there for long.

"That's possible, yes, but it's not any more or any less possible than it was at any other time prior to this moment, Raya," the doctor said. "It's just really impossible to make that kind of determination in memory loss cases. We don't know what's locked inside your brain, and what's not. It's really anyone's guess at this point. If you have hidden memories, they may or may not return. If they do return, it may be everything at once, or gradually over time. There's no way to predict if you have more hidden memories or not, and if so, when or if they'll return. It's just a mystery, unfortunately."

"A mystery. Just like everything else about this case. So many mysteries. Who did this? And why? Was I there when it happened? Did I see it? If not, where was I and why didn't I see it? If so, why don't I remember any of it? And the biggest mystery of all is ... does the killer know I exist, does he think I can I.D. him, and has he been hunting me for the past 20 years?"

Chapter 7

Dennis drove Dr. Forester home, and then returned to Raya's apartment. He and his wife spent the night, sleeping on the old hide-a-bed couch they'd been sitting on all evening. Raya tried to assure them that she didn't need them to babysit, but she didn't argue the point for long. After the stress of the day, it was comforting to know that she wouldn't be sleeping alone that night.

The next morning, after a quick breakfast, Dennis left for work, leaving Janet behind to spend the day with Raya. Not even two hours had passed before Raya's independent spirit took control.

"Mom, I can't thank you enough for running over here the minute I called, but I've lived alone and have been perfectly able to take care of myself since I moved out on my own at the age of 18. Nothing has changed, except that now I know a few things I didn't know before. I'm okay now. Really. You don't have to hang around. You have your life to get back to, and I have mine. In fact, I've got some deadlines to meet, and my client will have my hide if I don't have some blog posts ready to publish soon. Besides, you know I like being alone. So go on home. I'll be fine, seriously."

"Are you sure, honey? I don't mind staying, really. Nothing is more important than you. Everything else can wait."

Raya smiled and hugged her mother. "Thanks, Mom. But yes, I'm sure. I promise, if I need you, I'll call you."

"I'll have my phone on me all the time. Call if you need anything! Any time, day or night. Promise me you won't hesitate, no matter what."

"I promise, Mom. I tell you what. Call me as often as you'd like if you just need to 'check up on me', if that will make you feel better. And I promise to call every morning just to let you know I'm okay. All right?"

"Okay, honey, that's a deal," her mother said, hugging Raya tightly before leaving. "Talk to you soon!"

"Yep, mom, soon!"

As soon as the door closed behind her mother, Raya raced to her desk, sat down, and opened her laptop's browser. There was no doubt in Raya's mind which case would be the focus of her next blog series. Raya had a stake in this one, and nothing could stop her from seeing it through.

"I'm going to do everything I can to find out who you are, you freaking monster. And if I did see you that day, I'm betting I'll eventually remember. I'm a stubborn blogger, which is why my clients keep me around. They know I'll keep digging so I can make true crime interesting. One client even jokes that I'm the best 'grave blogger' she's ever hired. Know what's not a joke? Your rampage cost my family twenty years of peace. That's long enough. I'm coming for you now, and I'll keep digging until I find you. That's a promise."

Even though the crime was 20 years old, Raya knew she could count on finding a few bits of information on the Internet. Between Google and Bing, almost anything could be found if you knew how to use the advanced features of the search engines. Naturally, Raya's job as a blogger and her inherent geeky nature ensured that no web page could hide if she wanted to find it. However, even with a search pro at the keyboard, there wasn't much more information out there that she didn't already know.

"Ok, that was a bust, but I'm just getting started, you freak. Let's see. Here we go. maps.google.com. Driving directions... from Lafayette, La to St. Felicity, La ... and ... print. Next stop...St. Felicity Sheriff's office."

Chapter 8

After booking a cheap room at a Motel 6 about 10 minutes outside of St. Felicity, Raya threw two pairs of jeans, a couple of her favorite t-shirts, and a few essential personal items into a gym bag and headed out in her '98 Crown Vic Interceptor. It wasn't the sexiest car in the world, but she'd bought it at a police auction, and it was both reliable and powerful. Cops everywhere drove those cars for a reason and looks were never a factor. That suited Raya's practical, dependable nature just fine.

As she headed east on I-10, she found time to think about the turn her life had taken in just 24 hours. She knew she should be feeling anxious or fearful, but in all honesty, Raya was feeling amped up, filled with a sense of purpose and drive. Yesterday's revelations, especially the knowledge that she'd had her name changed and her life uprooted at such a young age, was like the lifting of the veil over the mirror that had mocked her for so long. Relief was mixed in with the energy, as she finally understood why she'd felt so distanced from herself all those years. It bothered Raya that her memory of that time was still shut off from her, but just knowing why made all the difference.

The drive along Interstate 10 looks the same from mile to mile, with nothing but trees lining each side with just paved road in-between. The trees block any view of the landscape beyond, so the scenery consists of only trees and road, road and trees. Like the Crown Vic, it didn't score points for beauty, but provided a reliable way to get from point A to point B, with plenty of time for plans to form.

I definitely need a plan, Raya thought. I've got to stay under cover as just a true crime blogger interested in an old, unsolved case. Mom and Dad spent 20 years making sure no one ever knew who we were or where we'd gone. I can't undo all of their efforts by blowing this. And yes, Mom, I know that you're going to have a fit when you realize what I'm doing, so you'll just have to forgive me if I fail to mention my whereabouts when we talk on the phone.

"Oh crap!" Raya said out loud, smacking the steering wheel with the butt of her hand. "I forgot to email Sherry, to let her know that I found a great old case to blog about." Picking up the smart phone lying on the passenger seat, she pressed #3 to speed dial her client.

"Sherry, hey, it's Raya. Yeah, I know, I was supposed to email you last night. I'm sorry. I got, um, caught up in some research I was doing on the next blog series I'm working on."

"Yep, I came across a cold case that has all the makings of a kick-ass series, so I'm headed out to do some investigative work right now. I'll be out of town for a couple of days, but of course, I've got my cell and my laptop if you need to get in touch. I'm hoping to have the first blog post ready for you to review within 3 days. Trust me; it'll be worth the wait. Talk to you later."

Whew, Raya thought, that was easy. Now if only I can pull off the ruse with Mom and the entire town of St. Felicity as easily, I'll consider myself an acting genius.

Cranking up the Adele CD she was playing, Raya let the rest of the drive along I-10 lull her into mindlessness. It was easy to drive on autopilot as Adele's raspy but powerful voice surrounded her with inspiration forged from pain. Raya didn't really relate to the songs in the same way that most women did. She'd never had a romantic relationship that meant enough to her to cause the soul-wrenching heartbreak that Adele sang about, but the pain of loss was something Raya understood, even if she'd never known why. Today, Adele's lyrics—which were moody and dark, but also strong and determined— held a different meaning for Raya.

The smart phone's Navigator, integrated through the car's sound system via Bluetooth, suddenly dimmed the sound of the song, overriding it with voice directions.

"Turn right at the next exit, in 400 feet," Viki announced. Raya had named the robotic female voice of the phone's GPS system Viki to give her a bit of personality that the phone's designers had failed to give her. Viki stood for Virtual Interactive Kinetic Initiator. When asked what that meant, Raya always grinned and replied, "Absolutely nothing. But it sounds cool, doesn't it?"

At the moment, however, Viki was reminding Raya that she was going to be in what she thought of now as "enemy territory" very soon. Turning the music down, she wanted to give full attention to her surroundings from this point onward. She'd be traveling back roads that curved and meandered as they followed the contours of the various bayous and rivers that permeated this area of South Louisiana. This was unfamiliar territory, so Raya wanted to make sure she missed as little as possible.

A good true crime blogger notices everything, she thought, so the story can be brought to life for the readers. That's what keeps the website popular, the client happy, and the roof over my head. And of course, it doesn't hurt to pay attention, so I don't end up as gator bait if I drive nose first into a bayou!

Chapter 9

Raya chuckled out loud at her little swamp joke, but she wasn't totally convinced that she wouldn't end up as gator food. The scenery had quickly changed. She was already deep into a world of bayou "camps". Raya, like most Louisiana natives, know that camps are the local Cajun term for what most people would call "cabins" or "summer homes" or even "dilapidated shacks". While the occasional camp might be quite nice, most were either old shacks with rusting tin roofs, or ancient travel trailers that had been converted into camps by adding rooms on in a helter-skelter fashion over the years. To outsiders, the little camps, looking as though they were going to be swallowed up by the surrounding swampland, represented a world completely foreign to them. To the locals, it was just a normal way of life.

Having grown up in Lafayette, Raya was no stranger to the unique landscape of Louisiana. Bayous weren't foreign to her nor were camps, but she'd never ventured this deep into the heart of the bayou, and she'd certainly never had to wonder if she'd find a killer at the end of the journey. Raya Landry considered herself a "tough cookie", but she had to admit that fear was beginning to drape itself around her much like the Spanish moss clung to the beautiful old cypress trees that grew all through the bayou waters.

"Shake it off, girl," Raya said to herself. "If those old trees can handle living in water, covered with what looks like a parasitic growth, then I can handle a quick trip to a town that may or may not contain a killer, who may or may not know anything at all about me, and who may or may not have any clue that I'm someone who doesn't even know if she's ever seen him." The convoluted spaghetti logic of that made Raya giggle, and the fear subsided - at least a little.

Just as she reached to turn up the music again, Viki broke the silence, causing Raya to jump in surprise. "300 feet ahead, turn right."

"Oh boy, here we go. It's showtime, folks!"

That right turn brought Raya into a very small town that nevertheless proudly proclaimed its friendly welcome with a sign that said "St. Felicity - Fun, Fishing, and Good Times".

Good times, huh? Well, I hope that's one prediction that actually comes true, she thought.

The posted speed limit was 25 MPH, so Raya could easily take in the sights. To the right, just past the Welcome sign, was Thibodeaux's Bait and Tackle Shop, with an old no-longer working gas pump in front, and a very old Coca-Cola machine right at the entrance. Despite its age, it apparently still worked, since a young boy, about 10 or 12 years old was feeding coins into the slot while propping his fishing pole against his shoulder.

On the left, across from the bait shop was Penny's Beauty Shop which looked like it shared a few parking spots and a front door with Olinde's Mortuary and Funeral Home. "Huh, I bet Penny styles the hair of the little blue-haired old ladies both in this life and beyond. That's convenient!"

Pulling up to what was probably the only stop sign in the entire town, Raya noticed a diner on the left corner, and the sheriff's station on the right. The white-brick building with letters stenciled on the glass doors that read "St. Felicity Sheriff" looked nearly deserted, which somehow made Raya feel better. A quiet police station probably meant St. Felicity didn't deal with murderous drama on a regular basis. Raya hoped that peaceful small-town vibe would keep her safe while she secretly hunted down the man who'd slaughtered an entire family, possibly right in front of her own eyes.

As Raya parked the car, she did a quick mental check of the approach she'd planned earlier, which involved finding someone "official" who'd agree to share some public details about the case, then start interviewing as many locals as possible who might remember the tragedy that took place 20 years ago.

Opening the door to the sheriff station, she noted that it looked like every other police station she'd ever visited. True crime blogging required interviewing local law enforcement officers wherever the crimes happened, so Raya had visited quite a few police stations in the last three years. Though somewhat smaller than most, St. Felicity's version had the same utilitarian old desks, beat-up chairs, ancient equipment, and a generally musky air that permeated everything. And like nearly every precinct, she was greeted by a sour-looking officer who probably hated the fact that higher-ranking suits thought he was only qualified to handle desk duty.

Officer Guidry, if the nametag on the desk was accurate, didn't even bother to speak. He just looked at her expectantly, waiting for her to get to the point of why she'd just stepped into his line of sight.

"Good morning, officer." Raya hoped her charming smile might loosen him up a little, but apparently it would take more than an attractive, girl-next-door personality to crack this one's "I could care less" attitude.

"My name is Raya Landry. I'm hoping to speak to someone about the Bayou Family Slaughter case."

Officer Guidry didn't even bother to hide the look of "here we go again", rolling his eyes, as he said, "Do you have new information that is pertinent to the case?"

"No, I don't. I'm writing about it and would like to get some official insight into it," she said.

"Sorry, lady, but this isn't a bar where customers can stroll in and ask the bartender for the dirt on the latest bit of gossip. The case you are so curious about is an open case, and we don't give 'official insight' on open cases to every pretty little gal that walks in here asking for it."

On most people, such a gruff brushoff probably worked for Officer Grumpy, as Raya now thought of him, but she wasn't your average, run of the mill "pretty little gal".

Adding even more sugary sweetness to the smile she shined upon him, Raya said, "Oh Officer Gru...Guidry, of course, I completely understand. Naturally, I don't expect to be given any sensitive details of the case, but I thought perhaps I could just take up a few tiny moments of someone's time to get just one or two quotes for my story. I'm sure our readers would find this town a much more likely place to spend their vacation dollars if they were assured that St. Felicity's elite law enforcement officers have done everything possible to protect its citizens from other crazed killers, over the years."

"Ma'am, I don't care if the President himself wants to know what we've done to protect our citizens, I ain't gonna bother our 'elite' officers with a request to talk to a stinkin' reporter. Now, go on, and..."

Guidry's grumbling was interrupted when a hand came to rest on his shoulder. That hand happened to belong to someone Raya guessed must be a detective. He obviously belonged here, but he was in street clothes, rather than a uniform, so deductive power of reasoning pegged him as a detective. He also happened to be young, attractive, and didn't look a bit grumpy. In fact, it looked as though he was trying to hide a laugh, as he spoke down—literally, since he was standing above the seated grump—to Officer Guidry.

"Officer, it's fine. I'm on my way to lunch, so how about I take Ms. ...?" He hesitated, implying he needed someone to fill him in on the visitor's name.

Quickly reaching out to shake his hand, Raya said, "Landry, sir. Raya Landry."

"Ms. Raya Landry. Interesting name. Raya, that is. Landry, not so much, since it's as common as white bread around here," he said, flashing a grin at her. "Anyway, Officer, like I was saying, I'm headed out to lunch, so how about I escort Ms. Landry out the door, and get her out of your hair. I'll be down at Berthelot's for my usual fried shrimp poboy, so unless the town is burning down, give me time to eat it before calling me back in this time. I don't want a repeat of yesterday. Shame that I had to let that sweet sandwich go to waste just to get Jimmy's dog to stop digging up Dub's turnips. Just because Dub is the Chief's pawpaw, ain't no reason to interrupt my poboy time, got it?"

Properly chastised, Officer Guidry grumbled, "Yeah, got it."

"Good man! Want me to bring a bite back for you?" he asked.

"No, Detective Simoneaux, thank you for offering but my Cheryl packed my lunch like always."

Raya noticed the change in the Officer Grumpy's tone. He actually was capable of polite conversation, though she still wondered what "his" Cheryl saw in him. She also noted that her initial conclusion was correct. The man who'd managed to affect this change in old Grump's attitude was indeed a detective, and she now had a name to attach to his wickedly infectious grin.

The detective opened the door, bent slightly at the waist, and made a sweeping gesture with his free arm, indicating that Raya should exit.

"Thank you so much for your assistance, Officer Guidry." With a final smile, Raya turned her back on him, and following Detective Simoneaux's invitation, she exited the building, with the detective following just behind.

"Sorry about the brushoff back there, Ms. Landry. I keep trying to get him to read a Miss Manners book, but for some reason, he just doesn't seem interested."

Raya laughed, saying, "No problem, Detective. I know you're on your way to lunch, so do you think perhaps you could spare just a second to steer me in the direction of someone in the department who might be willing to speak with me about an old case?"

"I'm sorry, Ms. Landry, but I guess you misunderstood. I'm not going to lunch, we are going to lunch. As in you and me. You have a full 30 minutes to pump me with questions, although at least 10 minutes of that time, I'll be happily stuffing my mouth. That would be your cue to talk, and mine to listen."

"Oh! I guess I did misunderstand. Thank you, Detective, thank you!"

"This way, then, Ms. Landry."

"Please, just call me Raya."

"Yes, ma'am, Raya it is, and since we're now on a first name basis, how about you call me Nick, since Detective Simoneaux is a mouthful. Save that mouthful for Berthelot's poboys, yeah?"

"Ok, Nick, it is," she said.

As they walked up the sidewalk, Raya decided she could possibly get more information out of Nick if she allowed him to flirt with her as he seemed to be doing. Besides, his wavy brown hair, deep tan, eyes that crinkled when he laughed, and that laid-back Cajun accent made it equally easy for her to flirt back. Whatever works, she thought.

"Berthelot's is just up ahead. It ain't the prettiest place in town, but they serve the best damned poboys anywhere on earth. I highly recommend the shrimp poboy, but the catfish plate is a great second choice," Nick said.

"I'm a sandwich kinda gal," Raya admitted. "I figure if you slap just about anything between bread, you've just created a great meal. So, if you say Berthelot's has the best poboys, then I'm game for that. Fried shrimp piled high between slices of crunchy-on-the-outside, soft on the inside French bread. Now that's a sandwich I'll never turn down."

"Excellent choice, and I'm happy to see somebody in this town is willing to take my advice. Seems to be rare these days."

They'd arrived at the front door of Berthelot's, though the door wasn't so much a door as it was an old wooden framed held together by equally old screen, which seemed to be awkwardly hanging from the doorframe on rusty hinges. But it was obvious why Berthelot's had chosen a screen door over a solid one. The insanely great smells wafting through that screen door was like a magnet pulling in anyone within 10 feet. Even if Nick hadn't recommended this place, Raya would have ended up here just from the enticing smell alone.

The interior matched the ambience of the screen door. It was a little dark, a lot old, and looked as though it might be held upright by carefully placed duct tape. Apparently, none of that mattered, since every table was full, and the diners looked as though they were eating in paradise.

Nick waved and smiled at one of the waitresses across the room, yelling, "Darlin', you think you can scare up a table for two for me?"

"Don't I always find a place for you, Nick?". That look they shared was one that was obviously filled with a history of flirtatious fun.

And just like that, the waitress whispered to a group of men sitting at a nearby table, at which point they all immediately moved to stools at the end of the bar. A quick flick of a towel across the table, and it was ready. "Here ya go, Nick. You ask and I deliver, right, chér?" Another sly grin, and she disappeared into the kitchen.

Once seated, Raya laughed and said, "I'm sure glad I'm with someone who can snap his fingers and get his way."

"Just comes with the territory, ma'am. That's what we 'elite' personnel do, ya know."

"Touché. Sorry, I guess I laid it on a little thick back there with Officer Grumpy. I didn't know anyone else was listening."

Nick leaned back in the chair, laughing loudly. "Officer Grumpy? That's your nickname for him? Ha! Love it!"

Raya's face reddened as she realized her slip. "Looks like I have to apologize again. I shouldn't be so disrespectful. I'm sure Officer Guidry is a fine officer."

"No ma'am, you don't need to apologize for that. In fact, you just made my day. Now, how about we get down to business before you say anything else you think you'll need to apologize for?"

"Shouldn't we order first?" Raya asked.

"Dani, hon, two shrimps, dressed, with a couple of sweet teas, yeah?" The waitress, whose name was apparently Dani, shouted from across the room where she'd reappeared from the back, "On its way, Nick!"

"You all right with sweet tea, Raya?" Nick asked.

"Sweet tea is perfect, thanks," she replied.

"Ok, good, now, we've ordered. Let's get to it. Why are you here, and what are you looking for?"

Nervousness threatened to overtake Raya, but she held it in check. "I'm a true crime blogger, and I'm planning to write a series of posts—which are similar to articles—about the Bayou Family Slaughter. You know, the old case from 20 years ago. I was hoping I could speak to someone in your department about the case. And yes, before you mention it, I understand that it's an open case, so there's not much you can share. But any information you can share would be useful to me."

"The Bayou Family Slaughter case. As luck would have it, that just happens to be a case I recently pulled from the files. And yeah, you're right, there's not much I can tell you, it being an open case and all. Still, I'm happy to answer questions if the answers are public knowledge anyway. But first I gotta ask something. What is a true crime blogger? My 12 year old cousin calls herself a blogger, and as far as I can tell, that means she writes a diary on the internet for everyone in the world to see. One day, it's like, "Oh Billy is so cute, and he actually looked at me!" and the next day, she'll write something like, "Billy gave his cupcake to Jenny. Oh, I'm so mad!". I'm guessing, though, that her style is probably a little different than yours?"

"Heh, yeah, a little bit. Basically, you can think me of as a cross between a journalist and a novelist. I research old crimes and report on them, much like a journalist would, but my blog posts are written in a style that resembles an interesting work of fiction more than a bland narrative of facts. The goal is to engage the website's readers with compelling posts that encourage them to return to the site again and again. And of course, there's always the hope that a retelling of a cold case will somehow help solve it, but that's not something that has ever actually happened, as far as I know. You never know, though, this might be the case that gets solved, all because I'm writing a series of posts on it!"

Chapter 10

Raya ignored Nick's chuckle. "I've read a little about the crime, and know the basic facts, but I'd like to hear more about the specifics, especially as it relates to what officers saw when they first arrived at the crime scene. Again, I do understand that you can only share details that are already public knowledge."

Dani set two large, frosty glasses of sweet tea on the table, along with a bowl of fresh roasted peanuts. "Your poboys will be out in a couple of minutes. Here're some peanuts to tide y'all over."

"Thanks a bunch, Dani," Nick said. "Much appreciated."

Cracking open a peanut shell, Nick returned his attention to Raya. "Keep in mind that I was only 9 years old when the murders took place, so obviously I can't give you a first-hand account of the crime scene from an officer's point of view. However, everybody and his dog heard all the details repeated over and over again, so I have pretty good second-hand knowledge of what went down. And of course, I've not only read the case files several times over the years, but as I mentioned earlier, I've gone over them very recently as well. So hopefully, you'll be able to get a pretty good idea of what the officers saw and felt that night.

The call came in at 8:30 p.m. that Friday night. Deputy Charlie Melancon was on duty and immediately recognized the address of the reported homicides. He called for all available backup to meet him at the mayor's house. He arrived at approximately the same time as Deputy Tim Johnson and Undersheriff Lance Hill. Together, they checked the grounds and then entered the residence. Once they were certain that the house was clear, they proceeded to examine the rooms that appeared to be the scenes of the crime.

From all accounts, it was a scene that nearly caused a few deputies to rethink their line of work. All law enforcement personnel see a lot of unpleasantness in our daily lives, but apparently, this crime scene was far worse than anything they'd ever experienced. And I'm not just referring to the obvious situation of seeing an entire family wiped out in their own home. That would have been within the realm of what we call 'normal'. No ma'am, what stunned the deputies that night was what that deviant had put that family through before he took their lives. That was one sick son of a bitch, pardon my language. He tortured each member of that family by playing mind games with them. We don't know all the twisted things he forced them to do, but he left behind enough evidence of the games he played that day to make it obvious that we weren't dealing with any ordinary homicidal maniac. So, even though I wasn't there to see that evidence, I know enough about it to tell you that the deputies were pretty messed up after seeing that crime scene. Yep. Pretty messed up for a long time."

Nick fell silent for a moment, and then quickly roused himself when Dani appeared with their orders. "Whoo, that looks good and smells even better! Dig in, Raya!"

The conversation consisted only of a few "yums" and grunts of approval while the two enjoyed the first few bites. Raya knew her time was limited, though, so as much as her taste buds wanted to continue the food fest, she had to take the time to keep the conversation going.

"These psychological mind games he played...are they a matter of public record? Can you talk about them?" she asked.

After wiping a bit of mayo from the corner of his mouth, Nick said, "Yes, the basic facts of the torture he put that family through are well known. You should go to the library later and ask Sue there to pull up the old newspaper accounts for you. They're on microfiche and you might have to dig through a lot of records, but just tell Sue which ones you want copies of, and she'll print them out for you. For a small fee, of course."

"Thanks, I'll do that. Where is the library?"

"You can see it from here actually. Look out that window there. See the little pale yellow building just down the road? That's it. Well, our 30 minutes are just about over. I'd say we have time for maybe one more question."

Raya thought quickly, and then decided to ask one that was most important to her. "In your opinion, Nick, do you think the killer was a local, and if so, do you think he is still living here?"

His pleasant demeanor darkened. He rose from the table, scraping the chair against the floor. Placing a $20 bill on the table, he shouted to Dani, "Thanks, Dani. Catch ya later."

"Sure thing, Nick. See you soon," Dani yelled back.

With that, Nick started walking out the door, and Raya hurried to catch up. Once outside, he turned to her and said, "Look, we don't know who the killer is. I have no idea if he was just some crazy lunatic from somewhere far away who just happened to be passing through our little town, or if he was my next door neighbor or the principal of the high school. Heck, it might not even be a "he" for all we know. So, I can't answer that question, but I can tell you this. If he was a local, I sure hope he's not still around. For everyone's sake.

I hope I was able to give you enough information, but if not, I'm afraid you'll have to find it elsewhere. I do have to get back so I can actually deal with present day crimes. Good luck with your blogging, Raya. It was very nice meeting you."

Without waiting for a response, Detective Nick Simoneaux walked away.

Chapter 11

Wow, I wonder why he turned so chilly all of a sudden, Raya thought. Oh well, at least he told me where to find more information before he completely shut down.

Five minutes later, Raya was scrolling through archived newspaper stories on the old-fashioned microfiche machine. Sue had helpfully led Raya to what the library called its "dungeon", and the nickname was certainly appropriate. The normal quiet of a library was loud in comparison to the solitude of being alone in the dungeon. Despite feeling silly, Raya turned her chair, so she was sitting catty-corner to the machine. It wasn't very comfortable, since her neck was at an awkward angle, but the thought of someone being able to sneak up behind her in this secluded space was just too unnerving. At this angle, she could spin through the articles on the screen, while still seeing anyone who might come into the room from the corner of her eye.

Although she knew the exact time frame to search through, the crime was so notorious that the reports about it continued for months. If her goal was merely to write a blog series on the crime, she would have focused squarely on the accounts that did the best job of summarizing the crime. However, this research was also personal.

I want to see if there's anything in these stories that might trigger a return of my memory from that day, she thought. Vague overviews might not be enough. I'd rather sit here for an extra 4 hours if it means uncovering one small nugget of information that makes all the difference in what I remember and what I don't.

Three hours and two blurry eyes later, Raya did notice someone out of the corner of her eye. Sue had come to let her know that the library would be closing for the night in just a few moments.

"Oh, but I'm not finished!" Raya said.

"If you know which articles you want me to print for you, tell me now. We have just enough time to do that. Then you can take them with you to read tonight, and you can return tomorrow morning if you need more."

"Thank you! I've been keeping a list. These are the ones I'd like to take with me tonight."

Minutes later, as Raya was paying for the copies, she asked Sue if she knew of anyone that might be willing to speak with her about the old case.

"Anyone in town over the age of 40, hon. They'd love to be able to share the grizzly story with someone new. Everyone else has already heard the story a million times so any time they get a willing ear to listen, they're more than happy to oblige. In fact, my momma's favorite pastime is talking. They call her Minnie Mouth. Minnie's her name, you see, and lord, can that woman talk. You want to hear everything there is to know about that terrible time, my momma would be the one to see. I'm taking her out to the flea market tomorrow morning. Meet us there, if you'd like. We'll be there first thing. Momma has it in her head that if she's not there when they open at 8:00 a.m., she'll miss the best junk. Then, you can make it back here by 10:00 when the library opens."

Raya fought the urge to give Sue a big bear hug. "That would be great, Sue. Thanks so much. Where is the flea market, anyway?"

"It's not hard to find. Just follow the main road here, for about 3 miles. When you get to Junction 42, hang a right, and you'll see it up ahead. I'll tell Momma you're coming. It'll give her something to look forward to tonight."

"Thanks again, Sue. See y'all tomorrow morning!" Raya said, as she gathered up the copies of the articles, and left the library. The sun had set, but the sky still held onto the faint light as if it didn't want to quite let go just yet. Raya was grateful for that. She wasn't exactly the type to be afraid of boogiemen or things that go bump in the night, but everything seemed to be just a little more frightening now that she was here, in this town, where a boogieman had once roamed...and maybe still did.

Stepping up the pace, Raya quickly arrived back at her car, which was still parked in front of the sheriff's office. Looking at the building now, she remembered the way Detective Nick Simoneaux had suddenly seemed to turn from friendly and flirty to annoyed or maybe even angry. *Not that it matters to me,* she mused, *but I wonder what I said or did that caused such an about-face.*

First things first, she decided, *I need to get to the motel so I can take a hot bath, then settle down to read all the newspaper articles I got from Sue. Then a good night's sleep will be just what I need to get me started bright and early with Minnie Mouth.*

Chapter 12

Grim Details Emerge About The Bayou Family Slaughter

Murder scene details from the Mayor's house have been leaked though they are sketchy still. According to anonymous sources at the scene of the crime, the murdered family's bodies were seated around the dining room table, with a complete dinner served and partially eaten. The adjoining living room had 12 white posters taped to the walls in a pattern we were told was reminiscent of the Stations of the Cross, a common ritual observed during Easter in Catholic churches. Apparently, every poster was numbered, sequentially, with each containing instructions aimed at forcing one of the family members to make a choice between two horrifying options. One example mentioned forcing Mrs. Alicia Broussard to choose between having her son or her daughter whipped across the back with a horse whip, for a total of 5 lashes. It appeared that if no choice was made, then both would be whipped with 10 lashes each.

Evidently, the choices became more brutal at each station, and included being forced to make decisions that involved beatings, dismemberments, and even sexual assault. Some of the choices were made by the adults, and some were made by the children, as evidenced by both the station instructions and the condition of the bodies.

When asked about these "choice stations", Sheriff Dupont declined to comment. "As you know," he said, "this is an ongoing investigation. We are doing everything we can to solve the case. We've called in forensic experts from Baton Rouge to help us process the evidence."

When asked if residents of St. Felicity and surrounding areas should be worried about the possibility of a serial killer preying on its citizens, the Sheriff replied, "We have no evidence that this is anything other than a one-time crime. However, whenever a tragedy such as this takes place, it's always a reminder that everyone should take precautions. Pay attention to your surroundings. Lock your doors, be cautious with strangers, and consider taking self-defense classes. Our department holds a free self-defense class 4 times a year at the old fairgrounds. If there is enough interest, we'll consider increasing the schedule as needed. Schedule information is posted on flyers located at the station, the library, and the post office."

Sheriff Dupont asked anyone with any information about this crime to contact his office as soon as possible. He stressed that anyone offering information can remain anonymous if they wish.

Just as Raya was reading the last paragraph of the newspaper article, she noticed her cell phone buzzing on the nightstand next to the hotel bed. Quickly she grabbed it, hoping it hadn't been buzzing without her noticing for long.

"Hello? Oh, hi Mom. Yes, I know, I'm sorry. I should have called you earlier. I've just been really busy with work today. No, really, I'm fine. I haven't remembered anything else from back then, and no more strange conversations have popped into my head. It's like yesterday never happened. Yes, I promise. I will. I'll call you if anything else happens like that. Thanks for checking in, Mom. I'll talk to you tomorrow. Love you!"

As Raya ended the call, she felt grateful that her mother cared enough to worry about her, and guilty for fudging the truth. She hadn't actually lied on the phone, but she'd left out the giant piece of information that she'd driven down to St. Felicity and was interviewing people about the case. That kind of news would have made her mother completely freak out.

So, really, I'm just making sure Mom doesn't worry, Raya thought. Yeah, right, it has nothing to do with the fact that I don't want to tell her what craziness I've jumped into. Well, crazy or not, I have more newspaper articles to read before I go to sleep. Tomorrow will be another busy day.

Chapter 13

The rest of the articles that Sue had printed for Raya were basically more of the same. None had any more details than the first had offered, but Raya had only managed to wade through the first week of articles before having to leave the library. She was hopeful that tomorrow's search would surface more details. So far, nothing had triggered any more jarring moments or memories. Raya wasn't sure if that was a good sign or a bad one, but at this point, she was going on the assumption that no news—r no shocking memories— was good news.

After such a long day, sleep came easily, despite everything on Raya's mind. The next morning, she felt almost excited at the prospect of meeting with "Minnie Mouth" and spending more time digging through old articles in the library.

A sane person probably wouldn't be excited about diving into this memory quicksand, she thought grimly. But then again, not many sane people are 'Grave Bloggers' either.

After a quick shower and a change into her standard jeans and purple t-shirt, Raya drove down the main street, hoping the town had a MickeyD's or BK that would allow her to grab a quick breakfast-on-the-go. When it was obvious that she wasn't going to be granted that wish, she pulled into Red's Gas-n-Go to see what she could find inside the little store. After entering, she was surprised at the selection of goods available. Every square inch of the place was packed with something useful - from toothpaste to hardware, and food to underwear. It was like someone had come along and miniaturized a Wal-Mart. There weren't many options to choose from in each category, but who needs 20 brands of breakfast pastries anyway, when you have bear claws and Poptarts to choose from? Grabbing her favorite, brown-sugar cinnamon frosted Poptarts, and a Diet Coke to ignite the brain, Raya strode up to the cash register and looked around for a cashier. No one seemed to be around. Anywhere. She'd been so amazed with the store's goods, she'd failed to realize how empty it was of people.

"Hellooo!" she called, in that sing-song way that people use when they are calling out to people who must be hiding somewhere.

"Oh, hi! Sorry, didn't hear anyone come in." An older woman popped up from under the counter, where she'd been apparently crouching to do who knows what down there. Raya tried not to giggle as she imagined the old woman reading her stash of Grampa Stud magazines under the counter.

"This is a great little store. I'm in a rush right now, but I'll have to come back later just to check out everything you have here," Raya said.

"We close at six every day, so as long as you get here by then, I'll be here."

Five minutes later, Raya had found the flea market, and after wiping the Poptart crumbs off her chest, she stepped out of the car and began to search for Sue and Minnie Mouth.

Chapter 14

"So did you get rid of that little annoyance?"

"What annoyance?"

"That reporter lady. What a pain, right? Kinda cute though, gotta admit. Those jeans...the way they hugged her ass was exactly the way I'd hug it, right?"

Guidry's face was a mixture of leer, sneer, and cheer, until Nick gave him a look that turned the sneer to fear.

"The lady wasn't an annoyance. She's just doing her job and our job is to serve the public, remember?"

"Right, right, yeah, um, well, I need to get this report finished." Guidry went back to pecking on the keyboard.

Heading back to his desk, Nick pressed a number on his cell phone's speed dial. "Perry, Nick here. Yeah, old man, you remember me. I'm the squirt you took potshots at every time I swiped satsumas off your tree. Ha! Good to talk to you too. Listen, I'm going fishing today, and I could use an ugly old coot to come along with me to scare the fish out of the water. Meet me at Shell Beach pier in an hour? Great! See you then."

The smile on Nick's face faded as he picked up the case file. This afternoon, he'd be fishing for more than bream and catfish. Today, he'd be trying to lure some information out of the man who'd treated him like a son since the day his own daddy disappeared. Nick used to pretend that Sheriff Andy Taylor from Mayberry was really Sheriff Perry Simoneaux, and Nick was cute little Opie. In reality, Perry was more like Frank Barone from the Everybody Loves Raymond sitcom, although Nick had been a little like Opie, minus the red hair and freckles. Nick didn't need anyone to give Perry a Father of the Year award though. Perry, his father's older brother, had been there for him when he needed him. That's why today was going to be tough. For the first time in 20 years, Nick was going to have to question what Perry knew about the Broussard family murders, and what role Nick's father had played in the crime.

Chapter 15

Just as Raya was wondering if she really needed the long wooden backscratcher with the plastic fingers that only cost 99 cents at the China Direct booth, flesh and bone fingers tapped her on the shoulder, causing her to jump, dropping the backscratcher, and very nearly knocking over the entire shelf of colorful dragons, Buddha statues, and paper fans.

"Oh, hi Sue, you scared me!" said Raya.

"Sorry about that. I said Hi first, but I guess you didn't hear me. Raya, this is my mother, Minnie. Mom, this is the blogger I was telling you about last night."

Raya grasped the older woman's hand in both of hers, saying, "Pleased to meet you, Miss Minnie." Minnie looked to be about 65 years old, in good shape, with smiling eyes and graying hair that refused to submit to the dark dye she had obviously tried taming it with.

"Nice to meet you too, Raya. That's such an interesting name. I don't think I've ever met anyone with that name before. It's like a ray of sunshine, isn't it, and it's just perfect for someone like you. Sue tells me you're like a reporter or something like that. What did you call her, Sue? Has something to do with the Internet, right? I don't mess with all that computer stuff, you know. Sure, everyone wants me to do that Facebook stuff and email and whatever other nonsense they use, but I just really don't see the point. If I want to talk to someone, I just talk to them, just like I'm talking to you right now. Why on earth would I need to do all that other stuff just to do what I already do?"

Raya understood Minnie's nickname now. She wasn't sure if she was supposed to respond to any or all of that, or which questions she should answer, but she soon realized that by the time she would think of what to say, Minnie would be on another subject by then anyway. So, Raya just smiled and nodded for the moment, waiting for an opportunity to steer Minnie towards the conversation she wanted to have.

"Momma," Sue said, "why don't we head towards the beignet booth, and you can tell Raya all about the Broussard murders 20 years ago? That's what Raya is investigating, and she can use your help with the story."

What a genius, Raya thought. Sue knew just how to manipulate Minnie into switching into the right gear.

As they walked, Minnie began telling the story as she knew it.

"You know how there's some events that you'll always remember, and you'll be able to say years later exactly where you were and what you were doing when it happened? Like the day Kennedy was assassinated or 9/11? Well, that's the same kind of event that happened here the day that Mayor Broussard and his family were killed in that awful, awful way.

Of course, we all heard about it that evening, just about the time everyone was sitting down for supper. The actual killings took place earlier that day though. Elgin, the coroner back then, said that Randy, Alicia and the kids probably died sometime around 3:00 that afternoon, but that it looked like they'd been tortured by that evil man for maybe an hour or more before he killed them.

My phone rang at exactly 5:22. I knew what time it was because I'd just checked the clock, since I didn't want my cornbread to burn in the oven. Anyway, I picked up the phone, and it was Rose, a dear friend of mine. She said, 'Minnie, did you hear what happened at the Broussard house?' She sounded like she'd been crying. 'Which Broussard's?' I asked her. She said to me, 'Mayor Broussard! I just heard from Doris—you know her son Bob is a deputy— anyway, Doris said Bob told her that Mayor Broussard and his whole family were murdered today!'

Well, I tell you, I nearly fainted right there. I mean, it's not like I was best friends with Randy or Alicia, but we'd all grown up together. We went to school together, attended the same church, saw each other at town functions, you know...all that sort of thing. The shock of hearing they'd all been murdered, even their little ones...well, it was just almost too much for me to stand.

Of course, once I caught my breath, I asked Rose how it had happened and if they'd caught whoever had done it. She said she didn't know much yet, but she did know that no one had any clue who the killer was. We promised to find out all we could from our other friends and keep each other informed. We hung up the phone then, and immediately started calling everyone we knew to either let them know what we'd heard or find out what they'd heard. There were lots of busy signals that evening, I tell you."

Minnie actually paused for a moment, obviously remembering back to that night.

"By the way, my cornbread did burn that night, but no one was really in the mood to eat anyway. Especially once we started hearing some of the horrible details of what happened to that poor family, food was the last thing any of us could stomach."

They'd all arrived at the beignet booth by now, and it was clear that food was probably not going to be something any of them would want to think about now either, so as if by silent agreement, they continued walking past it.

"My Henry, that was my husband, Sue's daddy, he was a volunteer firefighter. Well, back then, practically all the men were, so it's not like he was really anything special, you know. But still, it just made sense for him to head on over to the Broussard place, in case they needed his help with something. I told him to get over there and then let me know what was going on. I figured he'd be gone for a few hours, but I bet it wasn't more than 30 minutes after he left, he was back! I asked him, 'Did they make you leave or what?' He said, 'No honey, I couldn't stay. I saw more than I ever want to see in my whole life.' With that, he went into the bathroom and threw up. He meant what he said too. He gave back his volunteer fireman's badge, and never went near another disaster scene again."

Sue shook her head. "My daddy wasn't a wimp either. He served in the war. He was a hunter and had no problem dealing with the everyday problems of life. But he changed that day. He was never again that funny, silly man that everyone loved. Well, everyone still loved him, but he was just different after that."

"That must have been really hard," Raya said.

Minnie looked around at all the groups of people wandering around the flea market. Spreading her arms, she said, "It was hard for everyone here, Raya. That day changed everyone and everything. We all lost our innocence that day."

Chapter 16

When Nick arrived, he saw that Perry already had a line in the water and a can of Budweiser next to him, as he sat dangling his legs off the side of the pier.

"Hey old man, you're looking good," Nick said, giving Perry a light tap on the shoulder with his fist.

"Hasn't mattered how I look in years, Nick. Though I guess I never cared much about how I looked at any age."

"Anything biting?"

"Not yet. Turtle came along to take a nibble but that's about all. Grab a brew out of the ice chest there."

"Thanks, but I'm still on duty for another hour or so."

Nick sat, baited the hook on the pole he'd brought along, and cast it into the water beneath an old cypress. The two men fished in silence for a while, doing what fishermen do best. Smacking a mosquito that had landed on his arm, Nick finally got up the nerve to bring up the subject he'd been dreading.

"I've been asked to look into the old Broussard case," he said quietly.

Perry just raised his eyebrows and said, "Yeah?"

"Yeah. It's the first time I've had full access to the old case files. I guess I could have checked them out any time I wanted to really, but there never seemed any urgency to do so. But now, well, I've been digging into it pretty deep, and some things have come up as being kind of ... odd."

"Odd how, son?" Perry asked, in a tone that sounded as though he already knew the answer to his question.

"Well, I know I was just a kid when it all happened, but there seems to be some inconsistencies with some of the witness statements and how those accounts mesh with the way I remember things."

"You were just a boy, that's true, Nick. Is it possible that you're relying on inaccurate memories?"

"Sure, that's possible Perry, but if it's ok with you, I'd like to talk about some of those inconsistencies with you."

The two men locked eyes. Both understood that there was no turning back from the conversation to come.

"Ask your questions, Nick."

"According to the report, a possible suspect - or what we'd call a 'person of interest' today - was a man who had been seen driving a dark green sedan, make unknown, down Johnson Highway sometime around 4:15 that afternoon. The man was described as fitting the description of one Glen Simoneaux who was known to drive a dark green car that he would occasionally borrow from his brother, Perry. However, it was later ascertained that the brother had been in possession of the car during that time and could attest to the fact that he'd visited his brother Glen at his home that afternoon during the time in question. That the way you remember it, Perry?"

"If that's what the report said, then that's the way I remember it, Nick."

"Well, see, here's the thing, Perry. The day that happened was the same day that I woke up with a bad cold, or maybe it was the flu, I don't know. In any case, momma told me to stay home from school so I wouldn't get all the other kids sick. I was laying on the couch watching TV all afternoon. Daddy wasn't there by then, and I never saw you that day either. You see how I might wonder how those two things just don't fit, right?"

Perry stood, pulled the line out of the water, and prepared to leave. "Yep. I can see how that could be confusing. Guess somebody just isn't remembering everything exactly the way it happened. Hard to tell now, 20 years later."

Nick watched the man who'd raised him like a son shuffle down the pier, walking as though he'd aged 10 years in the last 10 minutes.

Chapter 17

"I read one of the news articles that mentioned the 12 posters lining the walls of the Broussard's living room, but there was only a brief mention of what was on them. Do you know what they were all about, Minnie?" Raya asked.

"Yes, we all know more than we ever want to know about those posters by now. You know, at the time something dramatic happens, you think you want to know all the details, but later, once you realize how terrible it all was, you wish you'd never been curious. You can't go back in time, though, and just erase the memories, now, can you?"

"Most of the time, that's true," Raya said. "Sometimes, though people do block out memories of terrible things." Raya's eyes stared out into the distance.

"I suppose you're right about that. I wish I'd blocked out the things I learned about that day. I need to sit down. Do you mind if we continue this conversation over on one of those benches?"

"Of course, I'm sorry. I shouldn't be wearing you out like this."

"Oh please, don't apologize." Once they were seated, Minnie continued. "The posters, yes. There were 12 of them, hung sequentially around the room. This is mostly a Catholic town, you know, so it immediately reminded everyone of the Stations of the Cross, but of course, that didn't fit with the fact that there are 14 Stations of the Cross. Still, even though the number was wrong, we all called them Stations anyway. It just seemed to fit somehow."

"Did the posters have anything religious written on them?" Raya asked.

"No, there was nothing religious about any of it, unless you count the fact that it was all just pure evil. There really was no reason for anyone to apply any religious meaning to any of it. Some did, anyway, though. In any case, you want to know what was on the posters. Naturally, I don't remember it all, but you'll find the exact wording in several of the news articles down in the library dungeon. They weren't published until much later, so that's probably why you haven't seen them yet.

Basically, on each poster was written an instruction. The instruction consisted of forcing one or more members of the family to make a choice. It was like one of those multiple choice quizzes they have in school, you know. But in this case, whoever had to make the choice had to select from either choice A or choice B, and if he or she didn't make a choice, then choice C would automatically be carried out - presumably by the killer.

Some of the examples I remember included one where Randy had to choose between having sex with his little girl or his little boy. Can you imagine being forced to make that choice? I mean, really, how could anyone make that decision? But if he didn't choose, then he and Alicia would be forced to watch the killer rape both children."

Raya bent over to place her head between her knees, because she could feel the light closing in on her, in the way she'd described when she felt faint.

"No! No! For God's sake, don't make him choose! Please, please stop this. Please!"

As the darkness retreated, and the world was light again, Raya realized Sue was kneeling in front of her, holding her by the shoulders.

"Raya, are you okay? Raya, talk to me!"

"Yes, yes, I'm okay, I think. I just felt a little faint, that's all. I'm okay now though."

"Stay right here, I'll go get you some water." Sue rushed off and Minnie placed her hand on top of Raya's.

"I'm sorry. I know how horrible it is to hear that. I should have warned you."

"It's okay, Minnie. I wanted to know. I assume all of the stations were just as horrifying?"

"Yes, unfortunately, they were. That wasn't even the worst of them. But the worst part of it all is that the poor family believed the killer would let them all go, if they only did what he said. In the end, he was a lying, evil sick bastard. Excuse my language."

Sue returned with a large cup of cold water. Raya took a few sips, and then said, "And even with all of that evidence left behind, they never figured out who did this?"

"No, to this day, no one has any idea. Maybe if all that CSI stuff you see on TV now had been available back then, it would have turned out differently. Who knows? I do know our little police force did all they could to solve the case. They worked on it for years and years. It still haunts them all - or at least the ones who are still living, anyway."

"Do you think any of the officers who worked the case would talk to me about it?"

"Maybe. Sue, when you and Raya head over to the library today, look up Ethan's phone number, and see if old Perry Simoneaux ever got a phone or not. If so, write that down for her too."

"Simoneaux? Is he related to Detective Nick Simoneaux?" Raya asked.

Sue answered, "Yes, Perry is Nick's uncle. He raised Nick after Nick's daddy took off. Momma, I'm pretty sure Perry has a phone these days, so I'll give Raya his and Ethan's numbers once I look them up."

"Minnie, I can't thank you enough for spending this time with me. If you don't mind, I would like to get to the library now, do that research, and then speak with either Ethan or Perry if they'll let me. If I can ever do anything in return for your generosity, you just let me know. Here's my card."

Minnie rested her hand on Raya's shoulder, saying, "I hope you get the information you're looking for, Raya, but I also hope you don't get more than you want."

Chapter 18

By the time Raya met up with Sue again at the library, Sue had the contact information for both Ethan Breaux and Perry Simoneaux ready.

"Ethan is the person I'd call first. He's a really nice man who spent years trying to solve that case. At the time of the murder, he was our Deputy Mayor, and also the parish tax assessor. I was told that after he was elected to succeed Mayor Broussard, he spent half of his time making sure Randy's pet projects continued, and the other half of his time searching for justice. I was too young to pay attention to any of that, but I didn't need to be an adult to appreciate his kindness.

Now, Perry Simoneaux, on the other hand is a whole different story. Granted, the man probably knows as much about the case as anyone in town, since he was the veteran detective back then, but I seriously doubt he'd share any of that information with you. I don't know why Momma suggested him, but she said to give you his number, so here it is. Just don't expect much from that old sourpuss."

"Thanks, Sue, for the numbers, and for filling me in on a little of what I should expect. You know, I'm actually a little tired, so I think I'm going to go back to my room for a while before I do any more research here."

"No problem, I understand. Hey, if you'd like, I can dig up a few articles that look promising, copy them, and have them waiting for you when you come back. As you can see, it can get pretty boring here, so it would give me something to pass the time."

"That would be extremely useful, Sue. Thank you!"

"No thanks needed, Raya. See you later."

By the time Raya arrived at her motel room, her anxiety had risen to a level that scared her. She found the card Dr. Forester had given her and dialed his office number. Luckily, the receptionist put the call right through to the doctor.

"Dr. Forester, this is Raya Landry."

"Raya, how are you?"

"Well, I had another brief episode today, and I'm a little shaken up, so I thought maybe I should call you. I'm sorry, I know you're probably really busy with real patients..."

"No, no, I'm not busy right now at all. Tell me what happened."

"Well, I've done a little more research and something I learned triggered a memory, I think. The same kind of thing happened where I felt faint, the darkness closed in on me, and I heard a woman's voice screaming, begging someone to not make 'him' choose. But the whole thing was over in just seconds. Still, it shook me up, I have to admit."

"Would you like me to come over, Raya? I can bring your mother along too, if you'd like. I think your dad is probably at work, but if you need him, I'm sure he'd find a way to get to you."

"No, no, I'm not home right now."

"Oh, well, why don't you come here to my office then?"

"I'm actually not in town right now."

No one spoke for what seemed like a very long time.

"Raya, may I ask where you are?"

Unable to lie, Raya admitted she'd traveled to St. Felicity to research and blog about the case, and to find answers to the past she'd forgotten.

"That's a very dangerous thing to do, Raya. We don't know what kind of reaction you'll have if more memories surface, and we don't know what that might lead to. You aren't safe there, at least not alone. Please come home. Or better yet, allow me to have your parents come get you."

"I appreciate your concern, really, I do, Doctor. But this is something I have to do. Please don't worry my parents. I promise to keep you informed about how I'm doing. Besides, I'm not really alone. Several very nice people, including a police detective, have offered to help. I'm in good hands, I'm sure."

"I'm sorry, but although I'm not officially your doctor, I just can't agree that being there alone is wise. Look, St. Felicity is my home town. As I mentioned, I'm not busy right now, and I could use a little vacation. If you insist on staying there, what if I came down, introduced you to a few people, and just hung around in case I'm needed?"

"I don't think I can afford to hire you, Doctor."

"I've been your unofficial doctor—slash—guardian your entire life, Raya, even if you weren't aware of it. You don't have to hire me. You're like family to me. If you'd like the protection of doctor-patient privacy, you can buy me dinner, and we'll call that payment for my services. Beyond that, I'll just be there as a family friend. I'll only pull out the doctor role if you need it. Deal?"

"That's extremely generous of you. It would actually be helpful to have you pave the way with some introductions as well."

"I'll just clear things up here, and head out. I assume you're staying at the one and only motel near town?"

"I am, yes."

"Great. I'll call you once I've arrived, and you can take me out to dinner. We'll discuss the plan of action then."

After hanging up the phone, Raya realized that all of her earlier anxiety has dissipated. Just having a normal conversation with Dr. Forester was enough to calm her down.

I don't know how I managed to get so lucky, but I'm really glad he's coming here. I'll have just enough time to rest a bit, then I'll go get the copies of the articles from Sue, but I'll wait to read them till Dr. Forester is here. Just in case there's anything in them that might set those memories in motion again.

Chapter 19

Jon Forester drove through the bayou as though he'd been driving these roads every day for the past 20 years. Progress had changed many things, but Jon's memories filled in all the details as though nothing was different at all. Where there'd once been rice and crawfish fields, there were now subdivisions filled with large brick homes, and sugarcane fields had made way for an occasional strip mall. But the bayous still wound themselves in and out of the modern landscape, refusing to be vanquished completely. Jon had driven these roads relentlessly as a youngster, so every curve held a memory.

Long before Jon had added a Dr. in front of his name, he'd simply been a boy who wanted nothing more than to escape the small town of St. Felicity and its rural ways. After school each day, he spent time in the library reading about the big cities that were just out of his reach. As he grew older, he worked as many odd jobs as he could so he could earn enough money to buy an old used car. The day he received his driver's license, he walked into Sam's car lot, handed Sam $350, and drove out in his freedom-mobile. Jon drove as far as he could as often as he could, just to get away from the town that had been choking him since birth.

Eventually, his good grades earned him a scholarship to LSU in Baton Rouge. Eight years later, just after receiving his license to practice medicine, Dr. Jon Forester received the call that forced him to make a difficult decision. His mother had suffered a stroke and needed someone to look after her. He'd considered just placing her in a home, but as much as he hated the idea of moving back to St. Felicity, he knew he'd never be happy walking away from his mother that way.

Five years later, his mother passed away, and Dr. Forester had just begun to consider moving away again when he'd gotten that call about the Broussard murders. He'd since assumed that the chance to move to Lafayette with Raya's family was just fate stepping in to help him find his place out in the larger world again. Now, as he drove towards St. Felicity for the first time in 20 years, Jon expected the old crushing feeling of his hometown would surround him yet again. He was surprised to realize, however, that he was looking at the old familiar landscape with fondness instead of anxiety. Perhaps age had played a part in this new feeling, or maybe the progress over the years had taken away just enough of the small town to make it more tolerable. In any case, by the time Jon rolled up to the motel on the outskirts of St. Felicity, he was looking forward to spending a little time there.

I wonder if anyone will remember me, he thought, or if I'll recognize anyone I grew up with. This must be how people feel just before attending class reunions, he mused.

After parking his car, he opened his old flip cell phone and dialed Raya's number.

"Hello?" Raya answered.

"Hi, Raya, it's Dr. Forester. I've just arrived at the motel. I'm in the parking lot. Do you want to meet with me now or later?"

"Oh Dr. Forester, let's get started now, if you don't mind. I can meet you outside, and we can walk over to Berthelot's to eat, if that's okay with you. I had the most delicious poboy there. I could eat there every day!"

"Berthelot's is still around, huh?" asked Jon. "Well, it had great food 20 years ago. Good to know it still does. I could use a nice hot poboy right about now. I'll be waiting here for you. See you in a few."

Jon watched as Raya strode purposefully towards him. It's amazing how resilient she is, he thought. That's one tough little lady. When Raya reached him, she smiled, shook his hand and said, "You know, I was thinking that we need to come up with a realistic cover story to explain both of us suddenly showing up here at the same time, including the fact that we already know each other. I mean, what are the odds of that being a coincidence?"

"You're right, Raya, I considered the same thing on the drive over. I think I have a simple enough story for us to remember. Let's say you and I met at an event hosted by one of my colleagues and his wife, who is also your client. When we chatted at the event, and you told me what you do for a living, I mentioned that I planned to be visiting my old home town that just happened to be the home of a mystery that you might be interested in writing about. You agreed that it was intriguing and decided to come down and check it out, and I would meet up with you if you were still here when I arrived. Does that sound like a plausible story?"

"Sure, that works. Let's get the names straight though. My client's name is Sherry. What's her fictitious husband's name – your colleague?"

"Let's go with Reese. That's unique enough to be believable, don't you think?" asked Jon.

"Reese it is, then. Now, I hear a poboy calling my name, Dr. Forester."

Jon smiled, saying, "Why don't you just call me Doc or Jon. Your choice. Dr. Forester just takes too long to say."

Raya stifled a giggle, and said with a smile, "It really does, doesn't it? Ok, I'd prefer to call you Doc. It just fits you better for some reason."

As Raya and Jon took a pleasant stroll towards Berthelot's, neither realized that someone was watching them from the window of Olinde's Mortuary, nor did they know that they'd just been chosen to play a deadly game.

Chapter 20

He'd only stopped into Olinde's for a moment to see if Sandra needed a ride home this evening. Her car had been acting up lately, and even though she'd worked as the receptionist / secretary at Olinde's Mortuary for 15 years, he knew she still didn't like being there alone. Sandra was known for being punctual; she always left work exactly at 5:00 p.m. The car's sporadic breakdowns had forced her to wait for a ride twice, and he hated the mood that caused! It came as a surprise, then, to see his old friend casually strolling down the street just at the moment he'd looked out the window of Olinde's elegant front door. Twenty years had gone by with no word from Jon, and now, at this moment, there he was with that woman he'd heard about. She'd been asking around about that day. He'd wondered if he needed to be concerned about her, but had mostly assumed she'd gather a few morbid facts, write a fluff piece for whatever rag she worked for, and then disappear like all the reporters before her. But now Jon was here, older but still looking much as he had in his college days. And he was with her. Why? Why now?

He'd spent the last 7,268 days with one thought at the forefront of his mind upon waking each morning. Today, I will not play the game. Today will not be like that day. Each day, for the last 7,268 days, dammit, he'd been good. He'd rejected the game that consumed his other mind. He said no to that mind Every.Single.Day. And now Jon was here, with that woman.

He'd be completely unable to reject the game now. He understood that one all-consuming fact as he watched them stroll so nonchalantly away. After 7,268 days, dammit, 7,268 days of being so strong and so good, they'd cancelled it all out. That other mind would not be put aside now.

So be it. The game begins. Again.

Chapter 21

Nick interrupted Officer Dan Guidry's moment of quiet reflection, which was a nice way of saying Dan was caught napping at his desk. "Dan!"

Officer Guidry flinched, startled awake. "Sheesh, Detective, you scared the crap out of me!"

"Good, I always said you were full of crap, Dan. We all benefit when some of that crap gets scared out of you."

Officer Guidry grunted in reply. "What can I do for you, Detective?"

"I plan to track down a few of the old busybodies around town today, to see if anyone remembers anything useful about the old Broussard family murder case. I'd also like to rummage through the old estate later today, so I'd appreciate it if you'd get authorization for me to do that."

Officer Guidry frowned, stroking his chin as he considered this request. "What makes you think that Ethan would authorize that after all these years? He's always been insistent that we honor Randy and his family by leaving the place alone. I know you were just a kid back then, but the press and curiosity seekers had turned the old place into a circus sideshow. Ethan bought it so he could stop the idiots from completely destroying the place, or as he put it, 'crapping all over a fine family's memory'."

"I know, Dan, but I'm not a reporter or some thrill seeker. Ethan wants to ensure respect for Mayor Broussard and his family, but I believe he also wants justice for them as well. So, use your charm, if you have any, Dan, and sweet-talk Ethan into letting me look around. You can assure him that I'll be completely respectful."

"Yeah, yeah, use my charm. All the gals around town know of my legendary charm. No problem, Detective."

Despite Officer Guidry's decided lack of charm, Nick knew he could be persuasive in spite of his gruff manner. He was confident that by the time he showed up at the old Broussard estate, the old house would be open and welcoming him into its sordid past.

As Nick left the station, he considered which old busybody would be first on his list today. Irma Crenshaw was the Broussard's maid and nanny back then, Nick thought. She was the one person who saw what went on in that house on a daily basis, probably going unnoticed during the most private of moments. She might know more than she even realizes about who might have had a grudge against the mayor or his family. Besides, he thought, Irma was pretty well known for her cooking skills, and a snack seemed like a really good idea right now. With a little luck, she'd have a few fresh warm cookies sitting on her kitchen table.

He knew exactly who he needed to speak to once he interviewed Irma, but he wasn't looking forward to it, so he hoped Irma's information—or food—would give him either an excuse to avoid talking to his momma, or the strength to do so. It didn't matter that Nick was a grown man now. Getting up the courage to speak to his mother about his father was not an easy thing to do.

Arriving at Irma's house, Nick noticed for the first time that it was falling into disrepair. The little Cajun cottage that he'd wandered past on his way to school every day was showing its age. The front porch steps were sagging, and it badly needed painting. Before he'd reached the front door, Irma was opening it.

"Nick! Don't you look handsome today! If I was just a few decades younger, I'd be telling all my girlfriends about the young man who'd come callin' on me!"

"Now, Ms. Irma," said Nick, "you know all the men in these parts would like nothing more than to call on you, but we all realize we aren't fit to keep company with a fine woman such as you!"

"Well, aren't you sweet, Nick. Would you like to share a cup of coffee with me? I have some snickerdoodles left over as well, if your belly can stand some."

"Ms. Irma, my belly is calling out for your cookies and coffee, indeed it is!" Smiling broadly, Nick followed Irma into the house and sat at her kitchen table while she poured them each a cup of coffee. "Help yourself to the cookies, Nick. How are you doing? Have you found someone to settle down with yet?"

Chuckling, Nick said, "Oh Ms. Irma, you know I haven't had much time to date, but I do keep my eyes open, just in case the right woman happens to cross my path. I promise you'll be the first to know if that happens."

"You have to make the time to date, Nick. Time won't wait for you. The years fly by, you know."

"Yes, ma'am, you're right about that. In fact, it's the long ago past that brought me here today. I was hoping we could chat about a time long gone."

"I'd be happy to, Nick. What part of the past are you referring to?"

"Well, Ms. Irma, I've been asked to reinvestigate the old Broussard family murders, and I hoped maybe you'd have some insights for me."

Nick watched as Ms. Irma's face lost its vibrancy. Folding her hands together, Irma leaned back in her chair and sighed.

"Some days, that time seems like so long ago, Nick… almost as if it was just something I read about in a book once, you know? Other days, I feel the hair on my neck rise, and it's as though it's happening all over again. Those are the days I look over my shoulder and wonder if maybe he's still here, watching me, watching all of us."

"Yes, ma'am, I understand what you mean. So, Ms. Irma, do you think 'he' is still around? Have you ever had a feeling in your gut that you might even know who he is?"

"There've been times, yes, of course, I've looked at one or another of the men in this town, and wondered…is it him? But it doesn't take long to realize that a girl could go crazy if she suspected every man in town. Eventually, I just had to stop wondering. It's the only way to stay sane and enjoy the life we're given, you know."

"Yes, ma'am, I suspect you're right about that." Nick allowed a moment of reflection before continuing.

"I know you spent a lot of time in the mayor's house back then, and I figure you probably knew more about the family than most of their friends did, am I right?"

Irma's eyes twinkled a little at the thought, and said, "Yes, Nick, people do tend to be blind to the help, don't they? They never really see us, unless they need us. We can be dusting just under their noses, and yet, it's as though we are just invisible. So, yes, I overheard quite a lot of private conversations that I probably wasn't supposed to hear. Of course, a good maid is a discreet maid, so I could be trusted to keep those private conversations private, naturally! Still, although I didn't gossip, I did retain the knowledge, yes sir, I did."

"Did you work for the family every day?"

"Only on weekdays. Mrs. Broussard liked to be a wife and mother on the weekends, so I was employed to cook, clean and watch the kids after school during the week, while she worked. So, of course, since it was a Saturday when 'that happened', I wasn't there. I've often wondered if things would have turned out differently if I had been. Perhaps I could have gotten help or even smacked him upside the head with a frying pan. I don't know."

"I'm just glad you weren't there, Ms. Irma. I'm happy you stayed safe and sound that day."

"Thank you, Nick. And yes, I know I probably couldn't have done anything to save that poor family that day. But I can't help but wonder sometimes."

"Yes, ma'am, that's understandable. If you don't mind my asking, was there anyone that you recall having a problem with Mayor Broussard back then? Or with Mrs. Broussard maybe? I know you don't want to gossip, but after 20 years, I think it's ok to share anything that might help me figure out who might have wanted to hurt them in such a terrible way. I'm hoping you may have some information tucked away in your memories that might shed some light on that."

"Well, of course, there's always someone who is at odds with a political figure. Mayor Broussard was well-liked, but he did have opponents who wanted to see him removed from office. Still, if it was one of them, they never succeeded in getting what they wanted."

"How do you mean, Ms. Irma? What makes you think they didn't get what they wanted?"

"Well, all of the mayor's pet projects were kept in place when Ethan Breaux was appointed to the office. He was determined to carry on with everything that Mr. Broussard had been planning, as a way to honor his memory. So, if an opponent was trying to block any of those projects, he didn't get what he wanted, that's for sure."

"I see. If it wasn't a political opponent who targeted the family, could it have been something more personal? Do you remember anyone arguing with either the mayor or his wife in the days leading up to the murders?"

"No, Nick, I don't recall anyone arguing. The mayor did seem—what's the right word—flustered, I guess. Yes, he seemed flustered Friday afternoon, just before I left for the evening."

"Really? How so? What made you think he was flustered?"

"Well, as I was gathering up my things to head home – my purse, for instance – I heard the phone being slammed down in the den. Slammed might be too strong a word to use. It's not like it was extremely loud, but it was a forceful sound. It was just noticeable enough to get my attention. I hesitated for a moment, and then the mayor rushed into the hallway, nearly running into me. He apologized, and quickly hurried on his way towards the back of the house. Even when the mayor was busy, he still always had an easy grace about him. There was nothing easy or graceful about him that day though. It was noticeable, but that tiny moment in time was definitely not enough to help me or the police solve the case, so I didn't mention it at the time."

"So, you had no idea who was on the other end of the phone?"

"No, not a clue. And other than that, I can't think of a living soul who would possibly have reason to do what was done to them. They were a decent family, all of them. I never saw them have any real issues with anyone on a personal level. I've always had to assume that the only thing that makes sense is that it was just some crazy stranger who randomly chose them for no rhyme or reason. Nothing else makes any sense to me at all."

"Well, Ms. Irma, I appreciate you taking the time to talk to me about this. I know it's not easy to relive those days. And I also appreciate the coffee and cookies. My belly is happy now, chér!"

"You come on by for snacks and coffee any time you want, Nick. I'm always happy to see you."

"I will, Ms. Irma. Oh, and by the way, I wonder if you'd mind if I practice my handyman skills over here sometime soon? I'd like to be ready in case I ever meet a pretty woman who is looking for a husband who can paint and fix things. So, if you wouldn't object, I could come over one weekend, slap a coat of paint on your house, and fix those front porch steps of yours. Who knows…maybe someone will see me workin' hard, and think I'd be just the man for her. Would that be ok with you?"

Irma giggled. "I'd be happy to let you practice your handyman skills here, Nick. Let me know what weekend you're coming, and I might even be able to arrange to have a few young ladies over for a meeting of some sort. I'm sure I can think of some excuse to lure them here."

"Thank you, Ms. Irma. I appreciate that. I'll let you know. It'll be soon, I promise. I should go now, but you have a wonderful day. Thanks again for everything."

Nick left, feeling as though he'd accomplished something. She didn't tell me anything concrete, he thought, but there's one thing that I know now that I didn't know before. The killer probably wasn't some crazy stranger who picked that family at random. I'd bet my badge that the person on the other end of that phone call was the killer – and that means the mayor knew him. Someone he knew, probably someone who lived in this town, and possibly still does, was the person on the other end of that phone. That narrowed the suspects down quite a bit, so Irma was much more helpful that she probably realized. It wasn't a lot to go on, but it was something.

With a full stomach and a little information, Nick was ready for the next interview of the day – his mother.

Chapter 22

Nick opened the old screen door, scanning the den for his mother. "Momma?" he called out. "Where y'at?"

"In the kitchen! Where else would I be at this time of day?"

As Nick entered the kitchen, Margaret Simoneaux was exiting it, wiping her hands on a kitchen towel, and the two collided. Nick wrapped his arms around his momma to keep her from falling and hugged her tightly.

"I'm sorry, Momma! Didn't mean to run you over."

"It's not the first time you've come barreling around the corner, Nick, and I'm sure it won't be the last. It's my own fault for not remembering that. What are you doing here in the middle of the day?"

"A guy can't visit his momma during the day anymore?"

"A guy can, yes, Nick, but you generally don't. You didn't get fired, now did you?"

"Now momma, you know better than that. No ma'am, I didn't get fired, and I didn't quit either. But truth be told, I did come here to talk to you about a case I'm working on. Do you have a few minutes?"

"A case, huh? Well, now, that's a first too. You never talk about your cases. Ah well, it must be important, or you wouldn't be here. Let me just turn the heat down a little on this pot of white beans. Then we'll have plenty of time to talk."

Margaret shooed her only son back into the den while she tended to the beans. Nick sat down in his daddy's old chair, nervously wondering how to bring up the subject, when Margaret joined him.

"Ok, what's on your mind, Nick?"

"Well, momma, I've been asked to look into the old Broussard case, and it's been made clear to me that I should leave no stone unturned when reexamining all the evidence."

"I'm surprised it took this long for them to put you on the case, Nick. You're the best detective this little town has ever had, and goodness knows, we need the best to finally put that terrible tragedy to rest."

"Yes, ma'am, I agree. It's time for the clouds to be lifted from above our heads, and there's one particular cloud that involves us. In the witness reports from back then, someone mentioned having seen Daddy driving near the old Broussard place, but there are conflicting reports about it. I was hoping maybe you could help me clear up the confusion where Daddy was concerned."

Holding his breath, Nick watched the emotions play across his mother's face.

After a moment of tense silence, Margaret let out a deep sigh. "I suppose it's time we talk about your Daddy, isn't it, Nick? You're a grown man now, who doesn't need the truth hidden from him anymore. In fact, I'm glad you're finally bringing him up. I've dreaded this day, but at the same time, I've wished it would come sooner rather than later, so I could get it over with, and just move on."

Nick rose from the old chair, crossed over to the sofa, and sat beside Margaret. "You're right, Momma, it is time. I can handle the truth, whatever it is."

Margaret fidgeted a bit before beginning. "I met your daddy under unusual circumstances. Having been born and raised in a small community—this town has grown a lot since I was a child—it was a given that everyone knew everyone else. Strangers didn't come to our end of the bayou very often, so if one showed up, everybody wanted their curiosity itch scratched, if you know what I mean. And your daddy, when he strode into town with his clothes dripping wet, and bits of moss clinging to his hair, now you can be sure there was a whole lot of curiosity about him! Glen was a handsome man, but you couldn't really tell from the way he looked that day.

I'd just begun walking home from Martha's house and as I came round the corner onto Grand Bayou Road, I nearly ran into him. He scared the daylights out of me, of course! I quickly backed up and started to run away from him, but I tripped over my own feet and fell right down. He bent down to help me up, but I imagined he was there to hurt me, so I let out a blood-curdling scream. Everyone within the sound of my voice came running, and before you know it, poor Glen had his face being ground into the road."

"Wow, Momma, I'm surprised I never heard about that," Nick said.

"Oh, it was so long ago, it's just become another little story that most have forgotten. Anyway, as I was brushing myself off, another wet stranger came running headlong into the crowd, and this one was definitely angry! He was flinging bodies left and right in his struggle to get to Glen. As you've probably guessed by now, that was none other than your Uncle Perry, and he was dead-set on rescuing his brother from the mob that was forming.

It was Mayor Randy who came along just in the nick of time to calm everyone down, in fact. He had Tommy Granger run off to bring back the Sheriff. In the meantime, he broke up the fight and took both Perry and Glen off to the side to have a little chat with them. Anyone that got too close to that conversation got the evil-eye stare from Randy, which was enough to keep everyone back. In due time, Randy escorted Perry and Glen over to where I'd been standing and told me that he'd like to introduce me to St. Felicity's newest residents. Glen apologized for scaring me and I think that was the moment I fell for your Daddy's charms."

Pursing her lips, Margaret said, "Now Nick, don't give me that look. Glen was charming; at least back then he was. Drinking—and memories—overshadowed that charm in later years."

"Did Daddy always drink like a fish? And why was he all wet to begin with that day?"

Margaret's hand covered her mouth as she giggled. "Glen was all wet because Perry had knocked him out of the pirogue when they'd been hauling in the trot lines. Apparently, Glen had said something that angered Perry, so Perry whacked him across the rear end with his paddle, sending Glen over the side and into the bayou.

Glen reached up from the water, grabbed a handful of Perry's shirt, and pulled him in beside him. The two fought each other as they sloshed up the bank to dry land. I guess Perry must have been winning that fight, because eventually Glen started running, and that's about the time he and I crossed paths.

To answer your second question…no, Glen didn't always drink so much. But the memories that drove him and his brother to our little town are the same ones that started the binges. Soon there weren't any more binges. Every minute of the day was just part of one long continuous binge. That's when he started getting mean, and that's the way you remember him best, unfortunately. I guess what they say is true. You can't run from your past. When your daddy realized that the memories of his past just followed him here, he tried to block them out with whiskey. But as it turned out, it wasn't just memories that followed him here. The day before the murders, Glen's past showed up at our door."

Nick felt his cell buzz a moment before it rang. "Just a second, Mom."

"Simoneaux."

"Detective, Ethan's agreed to meet at the house in 15 minutes. He'll only give you a short half-hour block of time and then the gates close."

"Damn. Ok thanks. On my way."

Margaret said, "I know you have to go. Don't stop to explain. We'll continue this conversation later." Kissing him on the cheek, she scooted Nick towards the door.

Chapter 23

Doc waved at a man leaving Berthelot's. "Ethan! Hold up!" As the man turned back towards their table, Raya noticed he looked rushed and perhaps annoyed at the interruption. He glanced at their table, scowled, and then looked over Doc's head as though searching for the person who'd called his name. With a sudden shake of his head, he looked back at Doc.

"Jon? You son of a bitch, it is you! Damn, man, how long has it been?"

Jon rose from the table and Ethan grasped his hand in both of his, pulling him into a bear hug.

"Ethan, too long my friend, far too long." Turning, Jon motioned to Raya. "Ethan, this is Raya Landry. She's a friend of a friend, and a blogger who is here to research and write about the Broussard case. I promised to show her around since we would be here at the same time. I hoped you could meet with her briefly at some point?"

Ethan smiled amiably. "Yes, of course, Jon, but only if you promise to have a drink with me before you and Ms. Landry leave town again."

"I'd love to, Ethan. Catch up on old times, right?"

"Absolutely. Well, coincidentally—and it is rather a strange coincidence—I was just on my way to the Broussard estate to meet with one of our detectives who is looking into the old case. I'm not sure if you remember the Simoneaux boy, Jon—his name is Nick—but he's St. Felicity's ace detective these days."

"I didn't know him well, but I'd heard about him from Raya, in fact. She spoke with him recently about the case."

Ethan looked surprised. "Really? Well, then, if you'd like to join me, we need to head over right away. I've agreed to let Detective Simoneaux examine the old place for a half hour only, and then I'm afraid I need to lock it back up. I'm going out of town for a short time."

Raya quickly gathered her things. "Thank you so much. I appreciate the chance to see the place." Her hands shook, but she turned her back towards the men, as she settled her nerves. Jon gently pressed her elbow with his reassuring touch.

"We'll follow you, Ethan, but don't worry about losing us. I remember the way."

Doc waited until he and Raya were driving away before he spoke again. "Raya, this may be a bad idea. We don't know what will happen when you see the Broussard estate. If you'd rather, we can turn around right now. I can see how nervous you are."

"I am, Doc. I won't lie about that. I'm not sure I can hold down the food we just ate. But nerves won't kill me. Not knowing what happened to me that day? That might kill me. So, nervous or not, let's do this while we have the chance. Apparently, this might be the only chance we get to visit the place. We can't ignore the one opportunity we have. We were lucky you saw Ethan when you did, or this opportunity might have passed us by."

"All right, Raya." Doc placed his hand over hers. "I'll be right by your side the entire time. If you have any memories, give me a sign. I'll know to watch you carefully and get you out of there if necessary."

"What kind of sign should I give?"

"Drop your purse on the ground. You and I will both reach down to pick it up, and I can have a chance to quietly find out what's going on with you."

"Why all the cloak and dagger stuff, Doc?"

"Never trust anyone in this town, Raya. Not a single soul. No one knows who you are. Your parents and I have kept your secret for 20 years for a reason. We need to make sure that secret stays hidden, especially while you are here in St. Felicity. If anyone realizes that you have memories of that day—that you were actually here—we lose the advantage of keeping your identity hidden. Please tell me you understand the importance of that, Raya."

"I do, Doc. I'm sorry, really, I do understand. I promise I won't take any risks. Cloak and dagger makes sense."

"Good. You'd better get ready then. The estate is just up ahead."

Chapter 24

It's a mixture of old South and new money, she thought. The driveway that was probably once created from crushed oyster shells, now long covered over with green grass, stretched in a straight path for what seemed like a mile. Along each side of the green beckoning drive were equally straight lines of pecan trees, row after row, like sentries guarding secrets of the past. Raya closed her eyes, waiting for the memories to flood her mind, but nothing happened. When she opened them again, Doc had pulled up next to Ethan's car, which was parked behind another. Nick had obviously been the first to arrive, and he and Ethan looked deep in conversation.

"Any memories yet, Raya?" Doc asked.

"Not yet, Doc. Let's see if we can shake some loose. Let's go."

Nick raised his eyebrows when Raya and another man ambled towards them. "Ms. Landry, I didn't realize I'd have the pleasure of seeing you here too. Ethan, you didn't mention there would be others here."

"Purely coincidence that I ran into my old friend and his acquaintance just as I was on my way here, Nick. I'm not sure if you remember Doctor Jon. You were still a boy when Jon left St. Felicity."

Jon shook Nick's hand, noticing that Nick's gaze was focused on Raya while he exchanged pleasantries. Apparently, there's some interest on Raya's part as well, thought Jon, since her gaze is locked with Nick's.

Ethan broke from the group and began walking towards the house. It was at that moment that Raya really noticed the once beautiful old house, now in need of paint and care and life.

"What a lovely house this must have been at one time," said Raya.

Ethan slowed, turned back towards the group, and said, "Yes, this was once a beautiful home filled with joy, but sooner or later we all learn the harsh lesson that neither happiness nor beauty lasts forever."

"Well, I don't know about that," said Nick. "Look into the soul of a woman who has lived a long and happy life, and you'll find the beauty and joy still hides within the lines and wrinkles she carries with her. You see those worn spots on the front porch steps? I'd bet they still hold the faint memories of all the kids who raced up and down on them. I remember the good times here, so some of that happiness and beauty must still be around, don't you think?"

"As poetic as that may be, Nick, those worn spots are nothing more than signs of age. If there are any memories residing in those front porch steps, they are the ones that quietly tiptoe into your darkest nightmares. Please, let's not waste time. I need to leave in 25 minutes, so come along now."

Nick nodded, moving quickly to catch up to Ethan, with Doc and Raya following quietly just behind. Raya was grateful to have Doc at her side, but she also felt safer knowing that Nick was here as well. If there was a boogeyman waiting for her here, she knew she wouldn't have to face him all alone.

Nick stealthily watched Raya while Ethan unlocked the door. She seems nervous, he thought. I didn't expect that from her. She investigates old crime scenes for a living, so I assumed she'd be relaxed, but her body is trembling slightly.

Once the old door was opened, Nick stepped back to let Doc and Raya follow Ethan inside. He noticed that Doc mirrored Raya's steps, as though he were her shadow – or as if they had a closer relationship than merely being a "friend of a friend". Nick scowled. Surely Raya can't be involved with someone old enough to be her father. Or maybe that's what this is, he thought. Maybe Doc is like a father to Raya, in the same way that Perry is a like a father to me. The thought of Perry made Nick's scowl deepen, when he realized that Ethan had apparently asked him a question and was waiting for an answer.

"I'm sorry, Ethan, I got lost in the past, I guess," said Nick. "What did you say?"

Ethan looked put out. "I said, where would you like to begin? The crime scene, of course, is through those doors, which leads to the connected dining and living rooms. Or would you prefer to start elsewhere?"

"Yes, of course, the crime scene is the best place to start. I know the way." Nick walked away from the group, hoping to have a moment to himself while he took in the rooms where the murders had occurred.

Ethan waited for Doc and Raya to follow Nick but was surprised to see Raya turning towards the staircase. "Aren't you interested in seeing the crime scene as well?" Ethan asked.

Raya hesitated. She let her eyes wander around the large foyer, glanced in the direction of the dining room entrance, and then turned back towards the staircase.

"Yes, I am, of course, but if it's okay with you, I'd like to see the area from a higher vantage point, just to get an overview of the area before I go in. Doc, would you join me as well?"

Doc placed his hand on Ethan's shoulder. "Ethan, we'll be right in, I promise. I know you're in a hurry to get on the road. We'll join you in a moment."

"Certainly, that's fine," said Ethan.

When Ethan entered the dining room, Doc and Raya climbed the staircase to the first landing. Leaning over the railing, Raya looked around at the entranceway below. Doc started to speak, but Raya held up her hand to silence him. He took the hint and leaned back against the wall to wait. Raya sat down on the first floor landing, grasped the carved spindles in her hands, and peered between them. Like before, the circle of darkness began to close in on her. The foyer below now looked like a scene being broadcast on a black and white TV.

"No!" She flung herself away from the railing when she heard the scream. Wild-eyed, she looked for an escape. Which way to run? Up or down? The door to the dining room below opened just enough to let a thin line of light shine through. Up! Now!

"Raya!" Doc whispered Raya's name but with an urgency that came through. "Raya, it's ok, I'm here. Look at me. Look in my eyes, Raya."

Doc was on one knee, holding Raya's face in his hands, forcing her to see him. Recognition slowly eased the panic in her face.

"Doc. Oh my God, Doc."

"You remembered something, Raya?"

"Yes, yes. It was just me seeing the room below, but not as it is right now. I was terrified. I know now that I was here, Doc. I was here, right here, on this landing, when they were in there. I don't remember all of it, but I know I was here. I need to get out of here now, Doc. Tell them I wasn't feeling well. Meet me at the car. Hurry!"

Before he could answer, Raya had run down the steps and out the door. Doc gave her a little time to make it back to the car, then descended the stairs and entered the dining room.

He'd been in these rooms before, many years ago, but decades of neglect had taken away the vibrancy he remembered. Jon knew he needed to check on Raya as soon as possible, but the sight of the scene of such a horrible crime, now stripped of its visible horror, still held him motionless for several moments. No blood stains remained. All evidence of the evil that had once inhabited this room had long been removed, but Jon could sense the unseen horrors pulsing from the walls, the floors, and the long, beautiful dining table. I'd never admit I feel such things, Jon thought. No one wants a doctor who relies on anything but the most scientific of evidence. But it's evident that the hair on my arms is standing on end. That's all the science I need at this moment.

Nick turned away from the far wall he'd been examining, facing Jon. "Where is Raya?"

"She got a bit of vertigo from looking down from the second floor. I sent her outside to get some fresh air. I'll go check on her in just a moment."

Ethan sighed. "You do understand that I don't have time to wait for her nerves to settle, don't you?"

"Yes, Ethan, I understand completely. It's fine. I'm sure she can write a credible blog post based on what she's seen and researched so far. We'll leave now, and let you lock up on time."

"Thank you, Jon. I appreciate your understanding. Detective? We have another few minutes. What else would you like to see?"

Nick looked around the adjoining living room and dining room. "If you don't mind, Mr. Breaux, I'd appreciate having the last few minutes to just look around this area on my own. Just a moment of quiet so that I can really 'see' what is not seeable."

"Of course, Detective. I'll be on the front porch. Meet me there in 5 minutes."

Chapter 25

Once Nick was alone, he let his mind take in the adjoining rooms as though seeing them from a great distance, allowing the "big picture" to settle down upon him. By not focusing on any specific details, Nick could often see the tiniest details that he would otherwise have missed. He stood in the middle of the two rooms, where they connected, turning around while glancing up and down throughout the movement. He quickly scanned the ceilings, walls, and floors, only seeing the furniture as blurred objects impeding his view of the rooms themselves. Next, he walked into the living room, and paced around the edge of the room, making the furniture the focus of his gaze, rather than the walls. Finally, he repeated the process in the dining room, focusing on the table and chairs.

Twenty years erases a lot, Nick thought, but evidence has a way of surviving the harshest of circumstances. A sealed environment like this abandoned house could be hiding a lot of missed evidence. I think it's time to call my old friend, Dustin. He may be Baton Rouge's craziest forensics expert, but his adventurous spirit doesn't conflict with his ability to ferret out the smallest of details. While I'm at it, I think I'll dig out the old posters from the evidence room, and let Dustin take a look at them. I wonder if anyone checked the scotch tape that the killer used to hang them on the walls? At that thought, Nick looked back at the living room walls, where the posters had once hung. For that matter, I wonder if anyone checked the paint on the walls where the tape had been torn away. He knew he didn't have time to inspect it any further right now. His few minutes were up, but he had ideas, and Nick was a man who could usually turn ideas into results. Today has been productive so far, he thought. I wonder if there are any other insights to discover before the day ends.

Stepping out onto the front porch, Nick saw Jon and Raya standing near their car. Nick could see that Raya's head was down and Jon looked concerned.

Ethan interrupted Nick's surveillance of the two, stepping around and behind Nick to lock the door. "Thank you, Detective, for sticking to my schedule. I hope you got what you needed while you were here."

Nick smiled and reached out to shake Ethan's hand. "Well, I didn't really expect to find much after 20 years, Ethan, but you know how it is. I needed to see it for myself. Uncle Perry used to tell me a story about a man that went missing. He'd always suspected the man had been eaten by a particularly ornery gator that he'd crossed paths with a few times, but it took several years for him to be able to catch that old beast. When a fellow officer asked him why he'd bother doing an autopsy on a gator years after the man went missing, Uncle Perry said, 'Just because a gator digested its victim years ago, doesn't mean you won't find the victim's watch ticking away in its belly when you slit it open, right?' So, I figured I might as well slit open this old house just to make sure there wasn't some scrap of evidence like a ticking watch lying around."

Raya lifted her head at the sound of Nick's voice on the porch. "Doc, don't worry, I'm ok now, really. I would like to head back to the motel if you don't mind though, because I think you and I need to talk about what just happened in there. Privately."

"I agree, Raya." Jon turned just as Nick approached them. "Detective, it was nice to meet you. Raya and I were just leaving."

"Yes, Jon, it was a pleasure to meet you as well. Raya? Are you feeling okay? Is there anything I can do?"

Raya thought the look of concern on Nick's face was genuine and surprising as well. "Thank you, Nick, but I'm feeling much better now. Just a little vertigo from looking over the stairway landing, I suppose. But I think I will head back to my room at the motel and relax a little, nevertheless."

"It's good to have a friendly doctor at your side, just in case, though, right?" Nick gave Jon a look that Jon thought he could interpret in more than one way. Nick is either warning me that I'd better take care of Raya, Jon thought, or he was making a snide remark about my relationship with Raya. I'm not sure which, but I don't want Nick asking too many questions right now.

"Don't worry, Detective. I'll make sure Raya is fine. I wouldn't want to face the wrath of our mutual friends if I let anything happen to her." Jon smiled and hoped his answer would satisfy Nick, although Nick's frown wasn't very reassuring.

Raya's cell phone rang, interrupting any further discussion that might have taken place. "Hello? Oh hi, Mom! Yes, yes, I'm fine. Well, actually, can I call you back in about an hour? I know, I'm sorry I didn't call sooner. I promise to fill you in on…everything. Just give me an hour, ok? Great, thanks, Mom. Love you!"

"Obviously that was my mother. Nick, if I don't see you again before I leave town, I want to thank you for all your help while I've been here."

Turning to Jon, Raya added, "Doc, can we go now? I'd really like to lie down for a bit before calling my mother back."

Nick watched as Doc and Raya drove away. Something is odd about those two, he thought. I can't put my finger on it, but there was a tension in the air, and I'd like to know what that was all about. In the meantime, I need to get back to the conversation I was having with my own mother. Afterwards, I'll look for those posters in the evidence locker, call Dustin to see if he'd be willing to do a little forensic side job for me, and then maybe I'll try to get some time with Raya alone this evening. Away from the watchful eye of Doctor Jon, I might be able to figure out what that tension was all about.

Chapter 26

On the way back to his mother's house, Nick tried to get Perry on the phone, but there was no answer. Odd, Nick thought. Perry rarely lets the phone ring more than twice before picking up. As private as he is, his time on the force trained him to always be on call and ready to roll if a call came in from the precinct. That training stayed with him, long after Perry retired. Nick decided he would call his uncle later, and if Perry still failed to answer, he would let worry have its way and begin a search for the old man.

Margaret was sitting on the porch, shelling peas, when Nick arrived. "Hi Momma," Nick said as he stooped to kiss her on the cheek. "Do you have time to finish the conversation we started earlier?"

"Do I look like I'm going anywhere, Nick? Go get a bowl, sit down, and help me shell these peas. Then I'll finish telling you about your daddy."

As a boy, Nick had hated shelling peas. It was a long, tedious, boring chore that only served to make him antsy to get away as soon as possible. Now, as a man, Nick looked back on those times with his mother with fondness. He hoped to share these quiet moments with her for years to come.

"I believe the last thing I mentioned this morning was that Glen's past showed up at our door, the day before the mayor and his family was murdered. Phillip, the mailman back then, knocked on our door that afternoon with one of those big brown envelopes in his hand, and it was addressed to your daddy. I was washing dishes at the time, so at first, I didn't notice your father's reaction, but the absolute quiet of the moment caught my attention. When I looked at Glen, he was standing there with something in his hands, staring at the contents of the envelope that he'd opened. I'd never seen that look on his face before. His eyes looked wild and panicked, like a fox that's been cornered, and I half expected the envelope to explode."

"What was in the envelope, Mom?"

"I'll get to that in a minute, son." Margaret dumped the bowl that she'd filled with peas into the paper bag beside her and started filling it up once again.

"I asked your daddy what was wrong. He didn't hear me at first, so I walked over to him, placed my hand on his arm, and asked again. That's when he realized I was there. He stared at me, dropped the envelope on the floor, and rushed into our bedroom. Of course, I picked it up to see who had sent it. That's when I knew that the life we'd been living would change forever."

"Momma, you know I love a good story, but please don't stretch this one out any longer. Who was the envelope from? What was in it? Why did it scare Daddy so much?"

"The return address was 1876 Angel Falls Drive, Bay St. Louis, Mississippi. It didn't have a name above the address, but it didn't need one. I knew that was the address of the so-called psychiatric hospital that your daddy had been in when he was between the ages of 12 and 16. That place was shut down before Glen arrived in town the day we met. That terrible place made the headlines for a short time, because the lady quack that ran the place was arrested and put in prison for conducting illegal and damaging psychological experiments. Glen never said much about his time there, but I uncovered enough to know that it was the cause of all his problems."

To avoid pestering his mother for the details of what was in the envelope, Nick emptied his bowl and scooped up more peapods that needed shelling.

"I wasn't sure what I should do, Nick." Margaret looked up into the clouds as though they might hold answers. "It wasn't my right to look inside the envelope, so I put it back on the floor, and went to the bedroom to see if I could do anything for Glen. I found him packing a suitcase, hurriedly throwing things in, without any regard to whether or not these were things he might actually need. I tried to stop him, but then he pulled that old Bowie knife out of his sock drawer. He just looked at it for a long time, and then looked at me with cold, dead eyes. I was afraid, Nick, and didn't know what else to do, so I left the house and walked into town. That was the last time I ever saw him, and then the next day...well, you know what happened that day. I often wish I'd taken the car to town that day, instead of walking. If your daddy hadn't had access to the car, no one could have seen him driving near the Broussard house the next day, could they?"

Nick set the bowl of peas on the porch, rose from the rocker, knelt beside Margaret, and gave her a long hug. Looking into her eyes, he said, "Momma, I don't want to ever hear you put even the tiniest bit of blame on yourself for anything that might or might not have happened with Daddy on that day. You were a saint to put up with that man's drunken tirades all those years, and I won't let you doubt your actions that day, you hear me, Momma?"

"I hear you, son, I do. I just wish things hadn't happened the way they did back then, that's all."

"We all wish that, Momma, I know. Do you mind if I ask you one more question?"

"I know what you plan to ask, sweet boy, and it's your job to ask it, so go right ahead."

Nick almost changed his mind, but he believed his mother understood. "Momma, do you think Daddy killed the mayor and his family that day?"

Margaret lowered her head, fighting back tears. "I don't know, son. I wish I could say that I didn't believe your daddy was capable of the horrors that took place that day, but I just don't know if that's true. Those eyes; the way he looked the day he left…anything is possible."

"Thank you for being honest with me. I appreciate that. And I know I said I only had one more question, but you never answered the one I asked earlier. What was in the envelope?"

"You are welcome to see it for yourself, if you'd like, Nick. It's still here, tucked away in the attic, behind that old chest against the back wall."

Chapter 27

The old shrimp boat had been partially buried in the swamp for so many years that it had become a part of the landscape. The bow and cabin remained above water as long as the river feeding into the adjacent bayous didn't reach flood stage. Nearby, cypress trees had grown up around the boat, shielding it mostly from view unless a fisherman needed to get close enough to untangle a line that he'd accidentally thrown into their branches. The stern and bilge had been firmly encased in the swampy bottom of the bayou, allowing the steel hull rusting away to form a new home for many of the bayou's underwater species. That same rust covered the entire visible portion above water, masking its presence even more, as the color of the rust combined with the original gray painted steel hull blended perfectly with the brown and gray tones of the surrounding cypress trees and the Spanish moss that draped over the old vessel.

If anyone bothered to look closely, they'd see that some parts of the deck above the water showed signs of occasional disturbance, shoeprints that slid through the moist layer of leaves, moss, and dirt covering the surface. He understood though that people were inherently too self-absorbed to take notice of small oddities within their surroundings, so he didn't obsess about leaving such traces when he came here. He knew he was careful enough, in that he always made sure no one was within sight when he boarded or disembarked.

Today, he arrived later than usual which didn't please him, but under the circumstances it was unavoidable. He preferred keeping to a strict schedule, as timing was as significant in his life as rules were. His mother always stressed the importance of three things: follow rules; be dependable; never be late. She used a combination of psychology and the power of games in both her work and in her role as a single mother. She'd understood the concepts of both gamification and game theory long before most.

In modern times, businesses have leapt upon the concept of gamification as a way to influence people to do tasks they'd not ordinarily choose to do. Because humans are predisposed to engaging in competitive games, applying that same concept to tasks people don't enjoy ensures that most of them will comply.

His mother often used gamification techniques to manipulate both her patients and her child into doing unpleasant tasks. She was primarily focused on the psychological aspects of her experiments, but she also excelled in mathematics. This interest led her to become one of the first to engage in the mathematical model of game theory, which studies the strategic decision making process. Game theory enables one to accurately predict behavior. By the time he'd reached adolescence, she had perfected the techniques of both gamification and game theory, allowing her to present carefully selected options to her subjects, presented within a rules and time based gaming format, in such a way that she could not only predict which choices the subjects would make, but she could manipulate them into making them willingly even if the choices would result in unpleasantness to the subject.

His own games always revolved around rules and timing, and over the years, he'd learned that humans were not only completely predictable but also very gullible. If they were given rules, they followed them, even if doing so would cause them great pain. Of course, they also always believed the lies that the game master told, in the hopes that as long as they followed the rules of the game, and kept within the stated time limits, they would receive the promised reward dangled in front of them.

Here, the damp musty odors of the forgotten boat reminded him of the early years, before his father died. Even at the age of two, he'd gone shrimping with his father at least twice a week. It was in this place, for the last 20 years, that he'd found the strength to deny the game. But today, arriving late, he'd broken a rule. As he looked around the cabin, he knew this would never be his safe place again. He'd just lost the one thing that enabled him to function out there in their world. He knelt down, crawled under the instrument panel, and curled into a fetal position, crying himself to sleep.

Chapter 28

Jon gave Raya some time to unwind before knocking on the door to her room. "Raya? Are you ready to talk?" Opening the door, Raya grabbed his arm, pulling him inside, and quickly closed the door.

"Doc, I was starting to freak out. I wasn't sure you'd ever get here, and I have to call my mother in a few minutes!"

Jon grasped her hands in his. "I'm here. We have time to talk a little, and get you calmed down before you have to speak to her. Sit down and tell me what's going on."

"I remember everything, Doc. I heard so many things that night, but I never really saw anything. I'm sorry, but I have no idea who killed them. I'm so sorry."

"Raya, Raya, there's nothing to be sorry about." "But I can't solve this!"

"No one ever expected you to, dear. It's not your job to solve this crime. The only thing any of us wants is for you to be able to deal with what you went through, that's all."

Cool tears fell from Raya's face, but her hands were trembling less, and her voice was growing steadier. "I guess I just fantasized that I could be the hero of this tragedy. I'd swoop in, remember everything, point my finger at the bad guy, and everyone would live happily ever after. What an idiot I am!"

"We all imagine those kinds of things once in a while, Raya. It's human nature. Actually, the things you do remember – the things you heard – they may actually end up helping Detective Simoneaux solve this case. You never know. If you're up to it, maybe we can meet with him later. First though, we need to make sure you are feeling well enough to speak with your mother. Do you think you can do that?"

"Yes, I think so. And I think it's time I tell her where I am. I shouldn't keep this from her any longer."

"I agree. If you'd like, I'll be happy to speak with her as well, to reassure her that you're not alone in this."

Raya jumped up and hugged Jon, taking him by surprise. "Thanks, Doc! Thank you so much for being here for me. I appreciate it so much."

Patting her back, Jon smiled. "I've been looking after you for 20 years, my dear. You just didn't know it. You're family to me."

An hour later, after finally convincing her parents that they didn't need to rush to her side, Raya hung up the phone, feeling exhausted. She groaned when she heard the knock on the door. "Doc, could you get that for me, please?"

Jon opened the door to find Nick's smile turn into a frown.

"Doctor. I didn't realize you would be here in Raya's room."

"Come on in, Detective. I was just leaving. Raya, if you need me, just call."

Jon left Nick standing in the doorway. "May I come in?"

"Of course, Nick, I'm sorry. Yes, of course." Raya stood and offered Nick a drink. "I don't have much here in the room, but I did pick up some Cokes last night. Want one?"

"No thank you, Raya. Actually, I was hoping I could convince you to go out with me tonight. There's a little place just outside of town that serves the coldest beer in the south and plays the warmest jazz you'll ever hear. The music is good, but not so loud that we can't hear ourselves talk."

Only after inviting Raya out, did Nick notice the slippers on her feet. "I apologize. I didn't even ask how you were feeling. I'm such an oaf. Please forgive me. Are you still feeling unwell?"

"I am a little tired, but I'm fine. Part of me wants to just curl up and stay in, but the other part of me is saying that a cold brew and good music will make me feel much better than an old motel bed and bad TV. So, yes, thanks Nick, I'd love to go out with you. I'll obviously need a little time to get ready though."

"No need to do anything other than put on some shoes, Raya. You look very nice. The dress code is always 'come as you are', anyway. But I do have to run an errand or two, so how about I leave and come back in an hour?"

Smiling, she said, "Perfect! See you then, Nick."

Chapter 29

Nick's smile didn't last long. Once again, Perry wasn't answering his phone. Dammit, Perry! Nick thought. I really don't have time to hunt you down, you old dog, but I need to see you before I meet Raya for dinner. Nick shoved his phone in his pocket and climbed into his truck. He looked again at the brown envelope he'd brought with him, now lying on the floor of the passenger seat. I don't know what the meaning is of that thing, but I have a strong feeling that Perry will know. Whatever that thing is, it may or may not solve this case, but finding out more about it will definitely answer a lot of questions about my father. Deciding to visit Perry's favorite haunts in order from closest to farthest away, Nick started with the Shell Beach pier, where they'd met just the other day. The pier was vacant, so he checked Perry's house, Berthelot's and Red's next. Wondering where to look next, he noticed Perry's Jeep parked on the street near Penny's Beauty Shop and Olinde's Funeral Home. Found you! Nick thought. Unsure which business Perry might be in, since both seemed unlikely spots for Perry to hang out, Nick flipped an imaginary coin in his head and chose Penny's to check out first.

Guess today is my lucky day, Nick mumbled to himself, when he opened the door to the beauty shop and saw Perry leaning over the counter in a deep conversation with Penny. "Uncle Perry! I thought I saw your jeep parked outside. You fixin' to get a perm and dye job, or is Penny making an appointment for you to get a mani-pedi?"

Perry scowled at Nick's jibes. "Watch your mouth, boy. You're not too old for me to put you over my knee."

"I'd like to see you try, old man!"

That finally brought a half-smile to Perry's face. "Were you looking for me, Nick, or did you just drop in to test your fighting skills against me?"

"I've been trying to find you for a while, actually. I was hunting you down when I noticed your jeep. Ms. Penny, would you mind if I stole him away for a few minutes?"

Penny brushed her graying hair back from her face as she smiled at Nick's handsome face. "Only if you promise to stop in now and then, Nick!"

"I promise, Ms. Penny. And I promise I won't keep Uncle Perry too long. I know you're waiting to put the rollers in his hair."

Perry smacked Nick's arm, making a loud thwacking noise. Laughing, the two of them walked out the door and headed towards Nick's truck.

"What's made you search high and low for me today, Nick?" Perry asked.

Nick reached into his truck and handed the envelope to Perry. "This. I need to know what this is, or more specifically, what it means." Nick watched Perry's face carefully as he opened the flap, but the only sign of recognition was from one slight upward movement of his uncle's eyebrows.

"The 3-sided dice. Where did you get this, Nick?"

"I'd rather you answered my question first. What is the significance of it?"

Perry looked around before answering, noticing Olinde's receptionist, Sandra, taking a smoke break just a few feet away. "Hey Sandra, I saw your daddy down at Berthelot's working on next week's sermon. He was almost finished so he'll probably be driving by soon. Just thought I'd better give you the heads-up."

After Sandra flicked the cigarette and rushed away, Perry turned to Nick. "Sucks to be a preacher's kid, I bet. I remember one time Reverend Harlan caught Sandra and her brother Tony dancing together. They were practicing so they wouldn't embarrass themselves if they ever found themselves at a dance. Of course, it was innocent as could be, but old Harlan tore into each of their hides for that. Even though little Sandra is all grown up now, I'd guess she is still a little afraid of her daddy. Anyway, Nick, let's talk in your truck. I'll tell you what little I know about it, but only in private. Let's cruise a little."

As soon as they drove away, Nick pushed Perry to open up.

"Your father had some issues as a teenager, Nick. Back then, psychiatry was going through a stage in which experimentation was encouraged and patient safety was of little concern. Doctors were given a lot of leeway in the treatments they used. Glen's rebellious 'bad boy' escapades eventually led to his being locked up in a state-run psychiatric facility in Mississippi that was especially active in its use of quackery and harmful experiments. He was there for nearly four years, until the hospital was closed down due to an investigation into its practices. The doctor in charge of the crazy experiments was sent to prison, and the patients were either released or sent to other facilities. Glen was released and came home.

For six months, he said very little to anyone. He reminded me of an empty cicada shell; just an abandoned exoskeleton with nothing inside. But the one thing he always had with him was a 3-sided dice – not this one, though. His was white and this one is red, but everything else about it is the same.

Of course, we all tried to break through his empty gaze, and eventually we did. Slowly, Glen began to reengage with the world, but his rebellious side was gone. In its place was a fear that stayed with him all his life. He learned to hide it from others – mostly – later in life, but it was never far away. And of course, alcohol became his drug of choice to help him dampen his fears, but it also made him mean, as you unfortunately know all too well. Anyway, about a year after he'd returned home, I finally managed to get him to tell me what the white, 3-sided dice was all about, although I'd asked many times before and gotten no reply.

That day, I found him standing under the old bridge near the high school. He was clenching something in his hand and staring out over the water. When he noticed me, he shoved his hand in his pocket, and when he removed his hand, I could see the familiar outline of that little dice pushing at the material of his pants. I took that opportunity to ask him about it again. I guess I picked the right time to ask, because he didn't even hesitate to answer.

Taking the dice back out of his pocket, he said, "This dice always defines my choices, Perry. Everything we do is a choice." Pointing to the side with the letter A on it, he explained, "This is choice A." Turning it, he said, "And this is choice B." He stopped explaining, so I asked him, "What's on the third side?" He looked at the letter X that was marked on the third side before answering me. "That's the choice someone else will make for me if I don't choose A or B."

"I never got any more information out of him about the dice, Nick, but he eventually stopped carrying it around with him. I never knew if he lost it or simply chose to put it away. So now I'd like you to answer my question, Nick. Where did you get this red 3-sided dice?"

"Momma gave it to me this morning. The mailman delivered it to Daddy the day before the Broussard murders took place."

Chapter 30

Dennis put his hands on Janet's shoulders, looking directly into her eyes. "Honey, maybe it's a good thing that Raya snuck off to St. Felicity. Now we all know that she didn't see the murders, she didn't see the killer, and most importantly, he didn't see her!"

"We don't know that for sure, Dennis. We don't know what he saw." Janet backed away, crossing her arms as though holding herself. She did that often when she worried about Raya, but Dennis knew how to calm her down.

"If she's not back in town by tomorrow, I promise we'll go get her. In the meantime, I think we need a double-chocolate malt with a shot of cherry juice. What do you think?"

Janet knew he was pulling that old distraction trick, but even when she noticed the mental sleight of hand, it still worked its magic. Smiling at the man she trusted most, she uncrossed her arms, grabbed her purse, and opened the door. "Well, what are you waiting for, Dennis? Those cherries won't jump into the chocolate all by themselves."

"Hon, what's that?" Dennis was pointing at something on the porch, just outside the door.

"Oh, did you order something Dennis?"

"Not that I remember," Dennis said.

"Huh, no return address, I wonder what it is." Janet ripped open the brown envelope, searching inside a nearly empty envelope. "Oh, here we go, it's something really small," she said.

"What is it, Janet?"

"Some sort of weird dice. A red, 3-sided dice," Janet said. Dennis examined it, noting the letters A, B, and X before slipping it into his pocket.

"I'll Google it later. Maybe it's a common prank being pulled on people these days," he said.

Chapter 31

Despite Nick's assurance that she looked fine, Raya spent the next half hour trying to decide what to wear. She'd packed light and had already worn two of the outfits she'd brought along. That left only two choices, really. She could wear the sleeveless jean jacket over her white t-shirt, and the straight-leg jeans with her favorite pair of Converse tennis shoes, or she could opt for the blue cotton sundress and sandals. Neither really seemed right for a date, but Raya wasn't sure if she should consider this a date or not. Nick had used the phrase "go out", which Raya usually thought of as a synonym for "date", but Nick's definition might be different. He's a natural flirt, she thought, which means that anything he says to a woman might sound like he's interested, when really, he's just being instinctively charming. Still, I think I'll wear the sundress and sandals, just in case he's hoping for a dinner date that shows some signs of femininity.

Just as she'd finished touching up her lips with a natural looking shade of light rose lipstick, Nick knocked on the door.

"Come in for a minute, Nick. I'm almost ready."

Nick handed her an envelope when he entered the room. "This was just outside your door. Your name is written on it, so it must be for you."

"Thanks for bringing it in. Odd. I wonder who would leave something here for me."

Raya opened the envelope and shook the contents out onto the bed. The red, 3-sided dice rolled several times, before coming to a stop. As she reached out to pick it up, Nick grabbed her arm. "Don't! Don't pick it up, Raya. Don't touch the envelope again either."

Raya looked first at the hand that was clasped around her forearm, and then stared at the concerned look on Nick's face.

"Why, Nick? What's wrong?"

Nick reached into his pocket and pulled out the dice his mother had given to him that day. "This is what's wrong, Raya. This dice – and the one laying there on the bed – might have been delivered by the person who killed the Broussards 20 years ago. That dice could be a threat to you, but if we're lucky, it might also yield the clue to the killer's identity. There's little hope that the one I have will still yield any viable fingerprints on it, but this one might."

"A threat to me?" Raya's hand instinctively covered her throat as though she could protect it from harm. "Why?"

"I don't know. Maybe your investigation uncovered something, and you don't even realize it. I might be jumping to false conclusions, as well, but it's certainly suspicious, so for now, I think it's best if we take precautions. I wouldn't want anything to happen to you, chér."

Raya no longer cared what Nick had meant by "going out". She decided to trust that the concern on his face was genuine, and that perhaps he cared a little for her. Tentatively, she placed her hand on his arm. "Nick, I'm scared. There are some things I think you should know. But I don't want to talk here. Could we please leave now and go where we'd planned?"

The fear in her eyes was all too real, causing Nick to catch his breath. "Yes, I'd like to get out of here as well. Let me just make some quick phone calls though." Nick phoned Officer Guidry, instructing him to meet them at Raya's motel room. "Come in your old truck, and don't wear your uniform. I don't want to alert anyone that anything is wrong, got it?" Next, he dialed his old CSI buddy. "Dustin, this is Nick Simoneaux. Yeah, it has been too long, you're right. Listen, old friend, I don't have a lot of time right now, and I really need your help. This is urgent. Could you meet me at our old hangout tonight? I'll explain everything when you get there. Thanks, see you there."

Nick carefully inserted the envelope and dice in one of the room's pillow cases, so he could deliver it to Dustin tonight. Once Officer Guidry arrived at the motel, Nick instructed him to keep an eye on the room and the surrounding area. "If anyone, and I mean anyone, tries to get into that room, call me, call for backup, and make an arrest. But Dan, be careful."

Nick hid the evidence under his shirt. "Raya, let's walk out to my truck as though we don't have a care in the world. I don't want anyone to think we have any suspicions. Can you do that?"

"I'm scared, Nick, but not too scared to pull myself together. No one will see my fear, I promise." And with that answer, she walked out the door, with Nick right behind her.

In the short time it took to drive to The Rusty Hitch, a run-down little bar about 20 minutes away, Raya had filled Nick in on the basic details, including her real name, and real interest in the case. "I'm sorry I kept you in the dark before, Nick, but we didn't want to take any chances. I hope you understand."

Nick's silence worried Raya, but he didn't keep her waiting long. "I had a hunch there was something you and Dr. Jon weren't telling me, Raya. I understand why you both kept silent about your identity. That made good sense. What didn't make good sense was your crazy idea to come here at all! How could your parents condone this trip? Surely they must have had more sense than you!"

"First of all, Nick, I felt it was extremely important for me to come here. I needed to be able to remember, can't you understand that? For the record, my parents didn't know I was here until this afternoon. They reacted in much the same way that you're reacting right now. But all of you need to understand that this was just something I had to do. You have no idea what it's like to have such a huge piece of your life ripped out of your memories. I didn't want to live the rest of my life wondering if there was some crazed killer searching for me or not. Today's revelation - when I remembered what I saw that day, and more importantly, what I didn't see – was disturbing but it gave me a little sense of relief as well. If I didn't see the killer, then perhaps the monster doesn't know I even exist. Surely you can understand why I'd need to come here now?"

Nick pulled into the hard-packed dirt parking lot of the old bar, cut the engine and turned to face Raya. "I'm sorry for chiding you, chér. You're right of course, and I would have done the same. But I've come to care some for you in the short time we've known each other, and I don't want to see you put yourself in danger. Your relief today might be misplaced, Raya." Nick patted the evidence still hidden under his shirt. "Maybe the killer didn't see you, maybe he did. All I know is that someone doesn't seem pleased to have you here and is bent on playing games with you. Games that are not fun, no doubt. Now that you have confided in me, could I please request that you not hide anything else from me in the future?"

"I know I'm not supposed to trust anyone in this town, Nick, but I do trust you. I promise I won't keep anything else from you." Both lingered a little longer in the old pickup's bench seat, unwilling to break the moment's connection, but neither was confident enough in the bond to question it further.

Fifteen minutes and one beer later, Dustin joined them at the table they'd chosen near the back door of The Rusty Hinge. "Ten bucks says you and your very attractive date didn't call me down here to get drunk and reminisce, old buddy. In fact, I'd be happy to triple the bet if it means you and I get to mix it up with a devil or two again. So, Nick, what kind of trouble are you and this lovely lady hoping to rope me into, huh?"

Chapter 32

From the window, she saw him pull into the parking lot. She knew she may not have completely rid herself of the smoky smell after scrubbing her hands in the ladies room, but if the odor was light enough, she could probably pass it off as second-hand smoke. He would be furious if she was seen smoking in public like a "common tramp". Her hands shook as she tried to scrub away the smell. She didn't want to think about how angry he would be if he knew, so she focused on calming down instead.

When she returned to her desk, she saw that he was speaking with Henshaw, a hearse driver who had been with the company for 40 years. He looked serious, but not angry; in fact, he appeared to be giving instructions to Henshaw, since Henshaw was nodding as if he understood. Noticing her approach, he dismissed the driver by turning his back on him and said, "Sandra, I'll be away for a few days. I'll call to check on you every night." Without giving her a chance to speak, he strode out the door.

Relief washed over her. He'd been at least 10 feet away from her, so any lingering smoke smell had probably not reached him. Since he wouldn't be home tonight, there'd be no need to rush home to shower. She smiled at the thought of being free from scrutiny for a few days. All I have to do now, she thought, is make sure I'm home when he calls each night. The rest of the time is mine to enjoy.

Chapter 33

After hearing Nick's summary of the current state of events surrounding the old case, Dustin was eager to get involved. "There's nothing I like better than a gruesome cold case, Nick." Realizing his gaffe, he apologized to Raya. "Sorry, Raya, I know it must sound crass of me to enjoy a tragedy that affected you so personally. I'm afraid I'm not the polished, genteel type, but I still should have been more considerate of your feelings. I hope you can forgive me."

"There is nothing to apologize for, Dustin. You and I are very much alike, in fact. I write about gruesome cold cases on a daily basis, and I would be the first to admit that I like it as well. This is the first time my job has affected me personally, so I don't even know how to react to it myself. But I figure if you enjoy the challenge, then you're probably the right person to be involved with this. I appreciate you taking some time to help Nick and I investigate this case."

Nick said, "Raya, you and I aren't going to be investigating this. You are going to get the hell out of St. Felicity, while Dustin and I do our jobs."

Dustin could feel the air literally being sucked out of the room as Raya's anger erupted. "Excuse me, Detective Simoneaux! But you don't have the right to tell me what I am going to do or where I am going to be!"

"It's Nick, Raya. I thought we'd gotten past the Detective Simoneaux stage by now". Softening his voice, he continued. "You're correct of course. I don't have the right to tell you what to do. But since you received that dice, I have to assume you are in danger here. That was probably a warning, and I hope you will listen to reason when I ask you – not tell you
– but ask you to please leave this town – and this case – in our hands. Dustin and I may have a chance at nailing this bastard, but it will be easier if we don't have to worry about your safety in the meantime. Please, Raya." Nick reached across the table to grasp Raya's hand. His touch matched his tone, assuring Raya that he was seriously concerned.

"I won't argue with your logic, Nick. I'll go home tomorrow afternoon, but I will continue my investigation from there. You have your job to do, and I have mine. I'll start by compiling the information I've already gathered so that I can submit the first blog post of the series to my client. That should give you two enough time to make some progress before I decide how I'll proceed with my own investigation." She gave Nick's hand a slight squeeze before removing it from his grasp. Smiling at both men, she said, "Isn't anyone going to get this girl a beer? This bottle isn't refilling itself, you know!"

Chapter 34

The next morning, Dustin unpacked the box of evidence he'd brought back to his private lab. He and Nick had stopped off at the station to retrieve the posters from the evidence room after leaving The Rusty Hinge the night before. Nick promised to get access to the Broussard house again as soon as possible so Dustin could process the scene of the crime as well. Until then, Dustin hoped to be able to come up with something from either the old crime scene posters or from the dice and envelope left at Raya's motel room door. Criminals usually believed they'd covered their tracks by simply wearing gloves, preventing their fingerprints from being discovered. But many forgot the other traces that are often left behind. They may have licked an envelope or stamp without thinking, or never noticed that a stray hair had found a hiding place amongst the evidence. Human DNA can be left on items in a number of ways, and Dustin frequently uncovered what other forensic processors missed. He owed his success rate not only to his skills in forensic science, but also to his inventive nature.

Nick usually described Dustin as a "crazy man with an adventurous spirit", but it was that same crazy sense of adventure that enabled Dustin to find new ways of thinking, new methods of testing, and better ways of analyzing evidence. It also didn't hurt that he was a self-made billionaire with the time and funds needed to create a beyond-the-state-of-the-art lab that not even the most well-funded government agency could afford. He'd created 3D laser scanners long before such equipment had been considered possible in our lifetime. These virtual reality scanners enabled investigators to "see" occurrences such as bullet trajectories and real-time blood spatter patterns. Even the simplest tools used daily by labs around the world had been reassessed and improved upon by Dustin. Every device and every procedure had been analyzed and reanalyzed numerous times over the years, until he'd found better ways to process every imaginable crime scene; even those deemed harshest to the preservation of evidence. It would be decades before the labs around the world would begin to use the types of instruments and electronic gadgetry that Dustin used on a daily basis.

Despite his reputation for brilliance in the forensics field, he was never high on the CSI job recruitment list. His reputation included the inability to get along with co-workers and a disdain towards authority. Dustin understood and followed the rules that mattered; sometimes to a fault. No one would ever question his careful, scientific methods or chain of custody follow-through. Such rules made scientific sense, but bureaucratic rules were nothing more than fuel for his rebellious and insubordinate antics. Despite his lone wolf reputation, he was the man others turned to when every other avenue had failed to produce results. He never charged for his services, but he only worked cases that resonated with him. Investigators considered themselves lucky if he chose to help with their case, as most were turned down repeatedly. Dustin would never turn down a case from Nick, however. His loyalty to Nick was forged years earlier. If Nick needed Dustin's help, he would always get it.

Dustin began by mounting one of the posters between two sheets of a clear polymer material that created a kind of negative pressure air pocket between them. This pocket could then suspend thin, lightweight items between them, in a way that resembles a magician's illusion. Once the item is suspended, a specially-designed set of molecular analysis instruments detect minute variances in its natural structure. These deviations were usually the result of some force or disturbance created by the handling of the item. The aberrations in the material are virtually undetectable without the instruments Dustin designed, but when analyzed in this way, evidence could sometimes be pulled seemingly from thin air. With twelve large pieces of poster board to work with, Dustin was optimistic about the chances of finding an anomaly that would point directly at a suspect.

While the first poster was being "scoped" as Dustin called it, he started the less-flashy analysis of the envelope delivered to Raya. When nothing useful surfaced from those standard forensic tests, he set the envelope with the remaining posters to be scoped later. He then repeated the standard tests on the dice without success. With no other tests to be run, Dustin knew it would all come down to the results from the posters and envelope being scoped. Since each test required up to an hour to run, and then more time for post-processing analysis, Dustin knew it would be a long day filled mostly with periods of waiting between moments of removing one item and feeding a new one into the machine. In the meantime, he thought, I'll check with Nick to see if he's managed to get access to the crime scene yet.

Chapter 35

Raya reached out to shake Jon's hand, but he pulled her into a warm embrace instead. "I'm a hugger," he said with a shrug, as he let her go. Raya stepped back, smiling.

"Doc, I can't thank you enough for everything you've done for me here. Actually, for watching over me all my life. Now that you aren't being kept a secret from me, I hope I'll see you at all our family gatherings."

"Well, maybe not all of them, Raya, but I'd love to see you and your parents more often now. In fact, I think you and I should both go to see your parents this evening. I need to stop by my house first to handle a few things and change into some clean clothes, but if you have the time, I'd like to pick you up at your place at six o'clock. I've already spoken with your parents, and they'd appreciate seeing us tonight so they can reassure themselves that you're still safe and sound."

"That works perfectly for me, actually. I'd planned to see them tonight anyway, but it would be so much easier if you were there with me, Doc. They trust you and your judgment, so if you assure them I'm fine, they'll believe it."

"Great, it's settled then. Have a safe trip home, Raya, and I'll see you at six tonight."

As Raya maneuvered the winding bayou roads, then later the long stretch of Interstate 10 which would take her back to the only home town she remembered, she thought of all that had occurred in just the last three days. For a woman who lived her life rooted in the concept of always being in control, it seemed astonishing that the past 72 hours had shown her just how little control she'd actually had over her own life for the last 20 years. Others had made life-altering decisions for her, some had hidden important information from her; and one heinous monster had used fear to wield ultimate control over Raya, her parents, and an entire town of people.

I can't change the past, she thought, but I can certainly take control over my future. The first step in making sure I remain in control of my own life is to figure out who disrupted it in the first place. I bet you think of yourself as the Gamemaster, don't you? For twenty years, you've controlled the game, but your time is up. I'll find out who you really are, and then it's game on. This "grave blogger" gamer will beat you at your own game. That's a promise!

That resolve left Raya feeling empowered. She'd rarely failed to achieve a goal once she'd made a firm resolution to it. This goal was far bigger and certainly more dangerous than any she'd attempted before, but she had two decades of lost time to make up for. She decided that alone had to give her the edge over the gamemaster.

When she arrived home, she took a few minutes to simply sit on the couch, feet propped up on the ottoman. Looking around, she began to see her style choices from a new perspective. Everything she'd chosen over the years reflected nothing of substance. Neutral colors, non-descript patterns, and items that were chosen for functionality over design permeated the place.

That old motel room had more personality than my own home does, she thought. Why did I never notice this before? Has my sense of self been so lost all these years that I couldn't even establish a sense of style? It's time to take control over that as well. When this is over, a shopping spree will be first on the list of things to do. It's time to bring myself out of hiding.

Chapter 36

He'd watched Raya's parents yesterday as they examined the game piece he'd left for them, and then as they got into their car and drove away. There was something familiar about them, but the fading light as evening approached, and the distance at which he'd positioned himself kept him from being able to see them in full detail. Today, that sense of familiarity nagged at him slightly, causing him to grow impatient and more nervous than he liked. Determined to stay in firm control throughout the game, he shifted his focus back to the next move he planned to make. Every move in the game was calculated beforehand. Each choice he gave to the players would be designed to not only inflict the most emotional or physical pain, but to also guarantee that the players would make the choices he wanted them to make. His mother had perfected that aspect of her games. She always knew exactly which choice her players would make, and she was never wrong. He, on the other hand, had not achieved that level of mastery in his previous attempts, but he was determined to do so this time.

He had eventually realized that his mother's success hinged upon two additional factors.

Lack of external stimuli was crucial. If the players believed there was no help available from the outside - that they truly only had two choices, with no possibility of another choice being presented from external sources - then he never had to worry that they would go completely off-script and make a third, unforeseeable choice.

Knowledge of the players' weaknesses was the second crucial factor. Preparation was needed for this before the game could begin. He had to know what each player feared most and what each player loved most. With those psychological weapons in hand, he knew any player could be manipulated into playing the game through to its conclusion.

It was all laid out in his mother's years of research. Time after time, she proved that the promise of reward or the fear of punishment provided all the ammunition needed. What she understood better than anyone, however, was that there was usually only one reward and one punishment that guaranteed success. All other rewards and punishments might hold the victims within her control for a time, but eventually, those promises and fears weren't important enough in the long run. Each person always has one thing for which they long for most, and one which they fear most. Their other desires and phobias hold some power over them but can eventually become less important than the desire to be freed from the game. For that reason, it is vital that he take the time know his victims' greatest wish and greatest fear before he rolls the dice for the first time.

He'd begun to deal with the problems of isolation and research. Arrangements were already being made to carry out the game in a place devoid of external stimuli; a place remote enough that the players would feel completely cut off from help of any kind. He'd confronted the main players with their first choices. He'd seen their reactions to the dice he'd left for them. He'd determined that young writer obviously had no courage as she was already running home to mommy and daddy.

Likewise, it was obvious that her dear parents were nitwits who had no clue that their daughter had unknowingly involved them in a game of choice, which of course, they'd have no option but to play.

He still needed time to deal with the preparation phase, however. Each player needed to be studied, analyzed, and researched so he could determine their ultimate weaknesses. Once the game formed in his mind, however, his ability to wait for it to begin would grow weaker with each day that passed. The moment he began to prepare, his lust to roll the dice started to grow stronger and stronger. He'd failed to finish preparations in the past because the lust had grown too strong. He'd failed to see the mayor and his wife make the final choices he'd scripted. In the end, he'd had to finish off the family himself, spoiling the game and nearly costing him his own freedom.

This time had to be different, he knew. This time, his lust for the game had to be rigidly controlled until all preparations had been completed, and every element was in place. He planned to use Sandra to control that lust. She would be his alternate game player while he made preparations. As long as he could take out his lust for the game on her, he could control his need to begin the real game.

It's almost a shame that I'll have to destroy Sandra in the process, he thought. She's been such a loyal pawn all these years, but collateral damage is necessary to ensure victory, and nothing is more important than winning.

Chapter 37

Henshaw stood on the far bank of the canal, watching over his sons and their sons as they inspected the fence they'd erected across the mouth of the canal. Henshaw had a large family, believing as he did that procreation was his purpose in life. His job as a hearse driver was only one of many. To support 16 children, he'd been many things to many people of this community. Over the years, he'd been a supplier of both game and seafood to the residents of the parish; he'd done manual labor for many of the chemical plants located in the area; and he'd worked on construction crews whenever the work was available. When each of his sons turned 10 years old, they became part of the family business. He taught them to hunt, fish, skin, dress, and prepare the game and seafood for trade. They became apprentices to his side jobs, quickly learning how to build, paint, maintain and repair everything including cars, houses, roads, and bridges.

Today, he watched his children, now grown with strapping boys of their own, do the work he'd finally grown too old to do. He'd been contracted to cut off access to the old Sashon canal from the main bayou. "Remy, boy, hang that sign on the middle pole. Everyone else, good job. Head on back to the house. Me and Remy'll meet you there, after we pick up them sacks of crawfish that Dub has waiting on us."

His sons and grandsons cranked up the small trolling motors that allowed them to move slowly through the marshy areas, propelling them back to the landing where their trucks and boat trailers waited for them. Once Remy finished nailing the sign to the pole, he paddled the boat to the bank, helped his old grandfather into the boat, and then followed his brothers, cousins and uncles to the landing.

Henshaw looked back at the fence as they slowly motored away. The sign read, "POSTED: PRIVATE CANAL. NO TRESPASSING." It had only taken one short conversation in the funeral home to arrange for the closure of this waterway that had served the public for at least 70 years of his memory. He'd never even questioned if the closure was legal or not. The pay was right, and who would question the man who'd hired him for the job, anyway?

Still, he would personally miss being able to fish here. One of his favorite spots for reeling in large sun perch had always been near that old shrimp boat that was now mostly hidden within the grove of cypress trees not far from the old Broussard place. He sometimes reminisced about the days when the Simoneaux boys, Perry and Glen, used to take that old shrimp boat they owned out for the day, usually coming home with a large haul of shrimp. Occasionally, they'd invite him to go out with him, but usually he was one of the men waiting to buy or trade for the shrimp they brought back.

A hurricane, whose name he'd forgotten long ago, had whipped the waterways into a raging frenzy one year, destroying the nearby camps, boats, and lives of many people. It was that hurricane that had somehow managed to move the Simoneaux's shrimp boat miles from where it was anchored to the place where it would finally deposit it there in the Sashon canal. Over time, the bow protruding from the canal had become just another part of the landscape, as nature grew up around it, creating natural cover. Very few people noticed it anymore and of those that did, only a handful really remembered who it had belonged to, or how it had ended up in a canal that was too shallow to have ever made it possible for the old boat to traverse. Now that access to the canal had been shut off, the memory of its existence would soon be forgotten by nearly everyone. Everyone except for the one person who'd hired Henshaw to erect the fence across the canal, of course.

Chapter 38

By the time Jon pulled up at Raya's apartment complex, he'd decided to try to talk her out of continuing her investigation. He thought she would probably resist the idea, but he hoped her parents would side with him tonight, and between the three of them, they could make her see reason. The fact that she was nervous about facing her parents tonight gave him a little confidence that she might be persuaded.

Raya answered the door looking anything but nervous. Her broad smile was followed by a tight hug. "Doc! Thanks for picking me up. I have lots of thoughts on the case that I want to share with you on the way to Mom and Dad's house." Grabbing her purse and keys, she was out the door and headed to his car, before Jon could even say hello. Once inside the car, Raya continued her stream of thought. "I realized while I was driving home this afternoon that I'd never gotten around to speaking with Nick's Uncle Perry. Remember, Ms. Minnie recommended that I talk to him, and even though Sue believed it might be fruitless, I trust Ms. Minnie's judgment. What do you think? Do you know Perry Simoneaux?"

Jon nodded. "Sure, I remember Perry. He and his brother Glen moved to town when they were in their late teens. Since very few people ever moved into St. Felicity, their arrival was noticed. Glen, Nick's father, was the dark, brooding type. Everyone was surprised that Margaret, Nick's mother, fell in love with him. I guess some women are just attracted to that type. Unfortunately, it didn't take long for Glen to start drinking, and that turned his darkness into violence. No one could prove it, but we all thought he might be abusing Margaret, and later on, abusing his son, Nick. But you know how that goes. The wives are usually too intimidated to speak out.

Now, Perry, on the other hand, was a quiet, thoughtful young man. He and I would occasionally have a beer together, and I came to think of him as a friend. We weren't really close, though. Neither of us discussed much more than the weather or sports when we ran into each other, but I always felt he was a straight-up kind of guy. By the time the murders took place, Perry had become the town's lead detective, so he would certainly have some insight into the case. I'm not sure he would be willing to speak with a stranger about it though, so I think it might be best if I approach him, rather than you."

"I appreciate that Doc, but really, I'd like to discuss it with him myself. If you don't mind, though, I might do a little name-dropping and mention that you are a close family friend of mine. That might get him to open up to me a little."

Doc turned into her parents' driveway and shut off the ignition. "We're here. We can discuss Perry later. Let's go face your parents now." Jon hoped that when the discussion of Perry came up again, he would have already accomplished his goal of getting Raya to agree to drop her investigation. If so, any discussion of who would speak with Perry would be a moot point.

Before Jon and Raya reached the front porch, Janet ran out the door, down the steps, and gathered Raya into a tight hug. "Raya! Thank God you're alright! We've been worried sick ever since we found out you'd gone to St. Felicity. After we're sure you're really okay, we'll probably be very mad at you, honey, but for right now, let me just make sure you're really here."

Laughing and pushing away from her mother's bear hug, Raya said, "Mom, it's fine. I didn't tell you because I knew how worried you would be. See? I was right. But I was very careful to keep my identity a secret, and Doc was there to watch over me. So, let's just go inside and talk about it."

Dennis stood in the doorway, clearly relieved to see his daughter was safe and sound. Raya noticed his features visibly soften as she climbed the front porch steps.

"Hi Daddy," she said as she reached up to kiss him on the cheek.

"Hi honey," he replied, stepping aside to let her and the others enter the house. As he swung the door closed, he thought he heard something outside. Curious, he looked around the yard but saw nothing moving. Probably just that old squirrel that keeps stealing the bird food from the feeder. He's a crafty little guy, that's for sure.

Janet walked towards the kitchen. "Make yourselves at home. Jon, would you like something to drink? We have cokes, water, and beer."

"Thanks, Janet. A beer would be perfect."

Once the four were settled in the living room, Dennis focused his gaze on Jon. "Thank you for taking care of Raya. It means the world to us to know that you were at her side. But it would have been nice, Jon, to have been told that the two of you were going to St. Felicity."

"Daddy, don't be mad at Doc. I wouldn't have agreed to meet him there if he'd told you I was going. It's my fault you were kept in the dark, not his."

Dennis shook his head. "I don't care whose fault it is. Neither of you should have gone to St. Felicity, and neither of you should have hidden it from us when you did. From now on, promise you won't put yourself in that kind of danger, and if you do, promise me you'll let us know where you are, Raya."

"I can't promise to stay away from St. Felicity, Dad, but I swear I'll let you know if and when I go back there."

As Janet, Dennis, and Jon all began speaking at once, each trying to convince Raya to stay away from St. Felicity, Raya stood up, speaking loudly so she could be heard over all the voices. "That's enough! I know you all have my best interests at heart, really, I understand that. But if your plan is to try to convince me to drop this investigation, forget about it. Even if I didn't have a job to do – and I do – I would still press on with this. All four of us have had our lives controlled by one maniac for the last twenty years! I am not going to let him control our actions for the rest of our lives. I just won't do it! Now, I plan to see this through, so each of you needs to decide right now. Either you're going to help me nail this bastard, or you're not. I'll love you no matter what you decide, but either way, I'm not stopping until that monster is found. I refuse to let him intimidate me, no matter what he leaves at my door!"

"What did you say?" Dennis looked from Raya to Janet and back to Raya. "What do you mean, 'no matter what he leaves at your door'?"

"Well, we aren't completely sure it was from him, but Nick – a detective in St. Felicity – believes the dice left at my door was probably from the killer. That means he's still there! We can find him, I know we can." Raya's eyes burned with intensity.

Janet gasped. Dennis stood, walked to the credenza near the front door, opened a small drawer, and picked something up. He quickly walked back to the living room and placed the red, 3-sided dice they'd received the day before on the coffee table.

"Is this the kind of dice someone left at your door, Raya?"

Jon and Raya stared in horror at the dice that lay there. "Oh my God. Daddy, where did you get that," Raya whispered.

Chapter 39

The memory returned. He hated that face. It stared at him every day, never looking away, always peering over his mother's shoulder while she berated him for making the wrong choice again. It was bad enough watching the dice spin again and again and again, but knowing those eyes were also watching, always staring, never wavering, made him want to rip that damned poster down from the wall, tear it into hundreds of pieces and shove them all down her wretched throat. But no, he could never do that.

Those eyes belonged to one of her favorite patients, the one she sometimes lovingly called Heathcliff. She spoke of him like she would the haunted romantic hero of Wuthering Heights. As if that sullen, useless, shell of a boy could possibly win her heart! No! Those eyes could never hold the love in his heart that he did. She'd see one day that he could play her game better than she ever imagined. She'd understand on that day that he was the true master of the game, not some demented soul she'd chained within her lab, to be poked and prodded. That face was nothing more than putty that she'd molded and formed as she'd wished, but it held no real power, no real mastery of choice.

He had no option but to listen to her while she chastised him and praised the other – for now. But the day would come when that face on the wall would no longer stare at him, and she would no longer be the master of the game. That day would one day come.

Chapter 40

Dennis rolled the dice between his fingers. "We found this on the front doorstep last night, in an envelope. I assumed it was some silly prank. I'd planned to search on Google today to see if it was some sort of crazy meme that was popular right now, but I just hadn't gotten around to it yet. Raya, is this the same kind of dice you received? And if so, why does that detective think it might be from the killer?"

Raya silently stared at the dice turning back and forth in her father's hand, unable to speak. Her mind threatened to shut down again, so she concentrated on the dice moving back and forth, refusing to let the light in the room be overtaken by the circle of darkness that wanted to consume her. Jon placed his hand on her back, not to hold her up, but merely to keep her tethered to reality. He spoke for her.

"Nick didn't say why he thought the dice might be from the killer. I plan to ask him that very question as soon as I can, though. But if there's even a remote chance that he's right, then we need to consider the possibility that our cover has been blown, and that we may all be that maniac's next target." Jon let that thought sink in before continuing. "It may be time for us to consider moving again."

"No!" Raya sprang from the couch, grabbed the dice from her father, and threw it across the room. "No! We are not moving again. We are not running. We are not hiding. No! Don't you see? With just a tiny red piece of plastic, he's managed to take control of all of us again! We cannot let him steal our lives from us again. I will not let that happen!"

Janet's trembling hands matched the shakiness in her voice. "Honey, we aren't equipped to deal with this. We can't fight that man. We're just normal, everyday people. If we don't leave, he'll kill us all."

Raya grasped her mother's hands in hers. "Mom, we can fight him. We have to! You've always said that I was the rock of this family. But I came from the two of you, and each of you has managed to remain strong for all these years, despite the tragedy you both had to deal with. I'm strong because you're strong. You and Daddy and I can beat this, and we have other people to help us too. Doc here, Nick, and others are all here for us. Together, we can build on the strength we already have within us. I can't run, Mom. I won't run."

Dennis wrapped his arms around his wife and daughter. "Raya, give me a few minutes with your mother."

"Sure, of course, Dad. I need to make a phone call anyway. Doc, would you come out to the back yard with me?"

Outside, Raya said, "Doc, I hope we can count on you, but I'll understand if you decide to leave."

"We're all in this together, Raya. We all run, or we all stay."

"Okay then. I'll call Nick now. He needs to know about this second dice."

Jon watched the way Raya held herself as she spoke with Nick. Every movement of her body, every expression on her face exuded determination and power. He could sense no fear in her at all. That might be her downfall, he thought. It's good to see her confidence, but a certain amount of fear is necessary to keep from blindly rushing into a viper's pit. I doubt I can dissuade her from following the path she's chosen, but I have to at least try to keep her from becoming over-confident. Jon watched Raya as she spoke on the phone. He turned and saw Dennis and Janet through the kitchen window, speaking to each other in what appeared to be hushed tones. He saw these three people as if from a distance, seeing them but not hearing them, in much the same way that he'd watched them for the last twenty years. He'd been a part of this family's life for two decades, and yet he'd been outside of their lives the entire time. Still, he thought, I think of these three people as family. Perhaps Raya is right. Together, maybe we can fight this.

"Doc? Doc!"

"I'm sorry, Raya, I didn't realize you were speaking to me."

"I spoke with Nick and told him about the dice left here yesterday. He's on his way. He asked us all to stay here until he gets here."

"Then that's what we'll do. And Raya?" "Yes?"

"I don't know if you're right or wrong to stay and fight, but either way, we'll fight together. Just promise me one thing. Promise you'll never underestimate that beast."

"Thank you, Doc. Having you on our side means the world to me, and I'm sure it does to Mom and Dad as well. And don't worry. I realize what we're up against, but we're smart. We'll plan. We'll prepare. We'll be ready."

Jon wished he could believe that anyone could be prepared for the kind of evil that had wrapped itself around the Broussard family twenty years ago.

Chapter 41

Nick dialed Dustin's phone the moment Raya ended the call. "Dustin, the situation has escalated. Want to take a trip to Lafayette with me?"

Dustin grabbed his keys and was halfway out the door as he replied. "You know I love a good road trip! I'll be waiting outside."

Within thirty minutes, both men were cruising down the highway. Dustin quickly summarized the tests he'd been running, letting Nick know that the results of the tests would be ready by the time he returned.

"Good," Nick said. "Apparently, we'll be able to get access to the house again tomorrow afternoon. You remember Dan?"

"Guidry? Yeah, sure. I always try to give him a hard time when I visit you at the station."

Nick ignored Dustin's grin, saying, "Yeah, well, Dan finally got in touch with Ethan. He manages the place. We'll have access by three tomorrow afternoon, for as long as we need. We just have to remember to lock up the place when we leave."

"Ok, now fill me in on what this little road trip is all about, Nick. Not that I need a reason to drive off into the sunset, but you did say the situation had escalated. So, what gives?"

"Remember those three-sided dice we showed you?"

"Sure, both looked like little red pyramids, with the letters A, B, and X on them."

"Well, if you remember, one was delivered to my father the day before the Broussard murders twenty years ago. That delivery was what caused him to leave, and he never came back. The other dice was left outside Raya's motel room door yesterday."

"Right, I remember all that, Nick. What's changed?"

"Raya called me from her parents' home in Lafayette just before I called you. That's where we're headed now."

"And? Why are we headed there?"

"She told me that another red, three-sided dice had been left at her parents' front door yesterday."

Dustin let out a long whistle. "Well, that must mean something. I'm not sure what, but whatever it means, it can't be good."

"I agree." Nick increased the car's speed to 85. "At this point, I have to assume that Raya is in very real danger, but I'm not completely sure why."

Dustin studied his old friend's face. He'd seen those brows come together in serious thought many times before, but he couldn't recall ever hearing that worried tone of voice that now accompanied Nick's look.

"Nick, is there something I should know about you and Raya? Haven't you only known her for a couple of days?"

"Yes, I've only known her for a short time, and no, there's nothing you should know about us. She's just a nice girl who may be in deep trouble if you and I take too long to do our jobs. Now, unless you want me to drop you off at the nearest motel so you can go watch sweet romantic Lifetime movies all day, I'd prefer to discuss the issues of the case."

Dustin held up his hands in mock surrender. "Right, Got it. Just the facts, man, I hear you. Ok, so the question of the moment is why. Why is Raya in danger?"

"The way I see it," Nick said, "either the killer is angry about some stranger asking questions and investigating the old case, or he knows who she really is. Either way could be bad for Raya, but if he thinks she's just some reporter, he may only be trying to scare her off. On the other hand, if he knows who she really is, he may be hell bent on getting rid of the one person who might have seen him that day."

"In either scenario, what's the point of involving her parents?"

"Good question, Dustin. I'm not sure, but maybe he just wants her to understand that she isn't safe even when she's not in St. Felicity. Or maybe he thinks that by threatening the people she loves, she'll be more willing to drop her investigation."

"I don't know Raya very well yet, Nick, but something tells me she's not the type that takes kindly to threats. She's what my grandma would call a 'pretty little thing', but I've seen sparks of defiance and determination erupt from her. I might be wrong, but if I was a gambler, I wouldn't bet on her running from a threat."

"That's my take on it too, and that means we need to figure this out before she runs headlong into shit so deep that we can't pull her out. I'm hoping I can convince her to go on vacation for a while. While I'm trying to knock some sense into her, I'd like you to try and get her parents to join us in persuading her to take off for a while."

"Your plan sounds a lot like an intervention. You really believe that you and I and her parents can gang up on her and convince her to take off to parts unknown while we hunt this guy down?"

"No, I really don't believe we can convince her to do anything she doesn't want to do. But we need to at least try, don't we?"

"If you say so, then sure, I'm game. Assuming she refuses to listen, what then? Is there a Plan B in that head of yours, Nick?"

Nick grinned. "I considered going all caveman on her and just dragging her off to some remote place in the middle of nowhere, but I have a feeling she'd claw my eyes out before we got out of the house. So, to answer your question, no, there's no Plan B. But when has that ever stopped us?"

Chapter 42

From this vantage point, he could see her parents clearly through the window. He found it amusing to watch people who believed that being inside their homes ensured their privacy. So often, they forget to close the drapes, and it never crosses their minds that the darkness outside only makes it easier to see them inside. It's like attending a play, where a bright stage light shines down upon the actors, giving the audience in the darkened theater a clear view of the action. Tonight's show was unlike a play, however, since he couldn't hear what her parents were saying, but he was unconcerned about that at the moment. He wanted to study their features and mannerisms. That nagging feeling of recognition continued to tug at him insistently, so he was determined to quiet it tonight.

Even with the clear view he had, he was still a little too far away to get a good look at the details of their faces. He needed to move closer, but he was as close as he could get without standing out in the open. He could hear Raya and Jon talking in the back yard.

If he moved closer to the house, he'd be standing in the front yard, where they couldn't see him but if they walked just a few feet to the left, they would have a clear view of most of the front yard. If he moved to the far side of the yard, he would remain obscured from their view no matter where they stood in the back yard, but he risked being too close to the busier street that ran along that side of the property. Which was the bigger risk? Being seen by Raya and Jon or being seen by random strangers driving by? Random strangers probably won't even remember seeing a man standing in some yard on a street corner, he decided, but Raya and Jon would definitely remember a man standing in her own parents' front yard.

Having made his decision, he stepped away from the hedge he'd crouched behind. Just as he began to walk towards the busy street, a car pulled into the driveway, its headlights swinging in his direction as it maneuvered beside Jon's car. Quickly, he retraced his steps and thrust himself behind the hedge once again. His heart pounding, he concentrated on controlling his breath, forcing himself to make as little noise as possible. Two car doors opened simultaneously, and he strained to see who emerged. He was surprised at the identity of the driver but did not recognize the passenger. Why would he have come here tonight? And who was the other man with him? This was a twist he'd not anticipated; one that did not fit neatly into his game plan.

The two men climbed the porch steps, and the driver knocked on the door. Through the window, he could see Raya's father move to answer it. Just before the door opened, the porch light turned on. He shifted slightly to the right, hoping to be able to see over the visitors' shoulders to get a better glimpse of the man's face. The door opened, and Raya's father greeted the two men. For just a moment, he looked out into the darkness as though he felt the presence of something watching him, and in that moment, his face was clearly visible. Raya Landry's father might be calling himself Dennis Landry these days, but that face belonged to someone else. That was the now older face of Daniel Broussard - Mayor Randy Broussard's brother; the brother of the man he'd killed twenty years ago. He no longer needed to see the wife's face more clearly. He now knew why she'd looked familiar to him before. Raya's mother was not Janet Landry.

Why had they both changed their names? Thinking back, he recalled hearing that they'd moved to New Orleans not long after the funerals. Yet here they were in Lafayette, using different names. Suddenly, it struck him that Raya wasn't just some random journalist – blogger, he corrected himself – digging into an old case. She was far more involved than she'd let on. Why had she lied? What did this mean, and how would this impact the game he'd planned?

The stream of questions rattled him. Tonight's shock at recognizing a face from his past reminded him of that day so long ago when he'd seen that face on the poster come alive, running down the street like a madman, wet with moss hanging from his limbs.

Chapter 43

He'd moved to St. Felicity within a week of his mother's incarceration. He'd stumbled upon the town when he'd inadvertently taken the wrong exit. The initial plan had been to drive straight through until he reached Houston, where he felt he could safely slip into obscurity within the teeming city. But fate and a flat tire had changed his plans. At the age of 19, he should have possessed the skills necessary to change a tire, but those weren't the sort of skills his mother had considered important. He was initially embarrassed when a man stopped to help. He felt like a fool, but the man was patient, acting as though it was perfectly normal for a young man to lack such basic knowledge. He explained each step of the process, and then let him try it himself. By the time he was ready to get back on the road, the man had invited him to dinner with his family.

That was the day he decided to stay in that little town, and it was the same day that he'd begun to think of Mayor Randy Broussard as his father. He'd never admit that to anyone, of course, but he spent the next two years as the mayor's apprentice. In the secret thoughts within his head, that apprenticeship led to his becoming a member of the Broussard family.

When his nemesis made his wild entrance that day, nearly three years since he'd last seen that face on his mother's poster, his fantasy world collided with the past he'd thought he'd escaped. One minute he was helping the mayor load old files into his truck, and the next he saw Margaret on the ground screaming up at the face he'd grown to despise. The face hadn't changed much. It even had the same look of despair and innocence as the photo on the wall of his old home. Later, he would not remember actually running from the truck to Margaret's side, nor the shouts and cries of the gathering crowd as he attempted to pound Glen's face into the pavement. The first thing he would recall later was the mayor grabbing him by the collar and yanking him off of Glen. He would remember the man he'd come to think of as his father scolding his actions in front of the gathered crowd, and then, turning his back on him, welcoming the boy and his brother to their town. He would think later, as he did so often, of the moment when the mayor introduced the boys to the crowd, and how he realized then that Randy Broussard was the one responsible for their arrival. He would never forget the conversations he heard that day; people praising the mayor for helping two young men, others clapping him on the back when they heard of his plans to mentor them. The hatred he'd always held for both his mother and that damned poster boy began to swell within him. This new seed of hatred would be directed at the Broussard family now; the family that had so easily shifted their allegiance from him to his old adversary, Glen Simoneaux.

For nine years, his hatred grew. He watched Glen court and marry Margaret; the very same woman he'd scared so badly that first day. He seethed in anger when they bore a son and began a family. He silently applauded when he heard the whispers of Glen's temper, and he smiled when the town's gossips speculated that his old rival was abusing his wife and son. And yet, despite the growing proof that Glen was not worthy, the mayor continued to treat both Simoneaux boys with respect. He promoted and backed Perry's appointment to lead detective on the small police force, while he encouraged the locals to buy shrimp from Glen even though they could purchase it cheaper elsewhere. The fact that his own position and standing in the town had been a direct result of the mayor's influence did not stem the anger that grew and multiplied with each imagined slight.

Yes, the day that he'd seen and recognized Glen was not so different than now, as he recognized the mayor's brother, twenty years later, hiding behind a new name in a different city. He didn't yet know what it all meant, but he could feel the seed of hatred stirring within him again.

Chapter 44

After gathering at the dining room table, Raya introduced Dennis, Janet, and Jon to Nick and Dustin. She then pointed to the envelope and dice displayed in the center of the table. "That's what Mom and Dad found at the front door last night." Nick bagged the evidence and handed it to Dustin.

"I'll compare this to the others, but it seems pretty obvious that they all come from the same source," Dustin said. "Still, one may hold a clue that the others don't, so nothing should ever be overlooked. I think we should consider interviewing the mailman who delivered the first dice to your father twenty years ago, Nick. He may know who mailed it in the first place. It's a long shot, of course, but it doesn't hurt to ask."

Raya glared at Nick, and then turned her attention back to Dustin. "What did you say? The first dice was delivered to Nick's father?"

Dustin grimaced. "Oops, was that not common knowledge?"

"No, apparently not!" Raya's voice raised an octave as she continued. "Nick, would you care to explain what any of this has to do with your father, and why I'm only hearing about this now?"

Nick wished he had warned Dustin to keep his father's involvement out of any conversations about the case, but now that it was out, he had to face it head on.

"I'm sorry, Raya. There are a number of facts about this case that we haven't discussed yet, and my father's involvement, if he had any involvement, is just one of those facts. I should have discussed it with you before now, but it just hadn't come up in conversation yet."

"Hadn't come up? You could have mentioned it when you showed me the dice in the first place! But now that the conversation has 'come up', I'd appreciate knowing the rest of the story." Raya sat, arms crossed in defiance, ignoring the uncomfortable silence around the table.

Nick explained that his father was a potential suspect in the case, describing everything he knew about his possible involvement. He tried to remember each detail, including Glen's time in the mental hospital, the original white dice he carried around with him after he was released, the subsequent alcohol abuse that led to his family problems, and the events that occurred the day before the murder.

"At this point, Raya, no one has heard from my father since that day. We don't know if he is dead or alive, or if he had anything to do with the murders. Obviously, we can't assume that being the recipient of the dice makes him guilty, since we would have to make the same assumption about you and your parents, now that you've also received the dice. I'm inclined to believe that the delivery of the dice caused my father to run away in fear, and that he isn't the man who killed your uncle and his family. But I know my father's temper all too well, so I can't rule him out as a suspect either. I promise you that his potential involvement in this case doesn't cloud my judgment. You have to trust me on that."

"It would be easier to trust you, Nick, if you hadn't kept that information from me. I trusted you enough to tell you my real identity. I assumed that when I promised I wouldn't hide anything from you again, that I could expect the same from you."

Janet said, "Raya, I'm sure Detective Simoneaux didn't mean to hide anything from you. He's just not used to sharing information about cases with civilians, right?" She looked at Nick, hoping he would pick up on her cue.

"That's true, Mrs. Landry," Nick replied. "It's just second nature to keep the facts of a case tightly controlled within the department." Turning to Raya, he said, "I hope you realize that I'm doing all I can to solve this case. I'm on your side, but I need you to trust that Dustin and I will handle this."

When Raya didn't reply, he decided now was as good a time as any to try to convince her to leave for a while. "Speaking of trusting us, I hope you will all trust my judgment on what I'm about to say next. I believe that you, Raya, as well as your parents, may be in very real danger. I can't imagine any other reason why you would have received the dice. In light of that, I hope I can convince each of you to leave town for a while. Take a vacation but don't share your destination with anyone but us. Stay safely tucked away while we find the person responsible. Can I count on you to do that?"

Raya's silence didn't last long. "I let you talk me into leaving St. Felicity yesterday, Nick, but I warned you then that I would continue my investigation. So, no, you cannot count on me to run and hide now. Mom, Dad, Doc, and I have all discussed this. We aren't going to let our lives be controlled any longer. We're all in this together, Nick, like it or not, so it's time to just accept that. Got it?"

Nick sighed and shrugged his shoulders. "Got it. Fine, if we can't convince you to leave, then we need to pool our information, discuss strategies, and make sure we're all on the same page. We share everything we know, and everything we think might have the slightest relevance with each other, but we keep these conversations confined to the people in this room. Are we all agreed on that?"

Nick made sure everyone understood and agreed before continuing. "Raya, what do you think about publishing your first blog post about the case tomorrow? I'm thinking your story might be the bait we need to lure this guy out of hiding, hopefully right into a trap we set for him."

Now that Nick was actively involving Raya in the investigation, she was able to release the animosity that had held her body rigid for the past few minutes. Resolve and excitement took its place. "I'd planned to submit my first post about the case tomorrow anyway, so that won't be a problem at all. Is there any particular aspect you think I should focus on? What bait should I throw out, Nick?"

The six of them discussed their strategy for the next several hours, finally breaking up the meeting at two in the morning. Nick drove Dustin home so he could review the tests that had finished running hours earlier. Dustin promised to give Nick a few hours to sleep before calling him with the results. Both men hoped the plans they'd devised wouldn't backfire on them because the lives of people they'd recently come to care about were at stake.

Chapter 45

Raya woke the next morning filled with energy, despite having only slept four hours. While she waited for the Eggos to pop up from the toaster, she sent a quick email to Sherry to let her know that she would write and submit the first blog post of the new crime series today. She thought back to the plans they'd made the night before. Despite Nick's continual – and occasionally annoying – warning, she felt they had a real shot of drawing the killer out once she put the first step of the plan into motion. We've already captured his attention, she thought. Now all we have to do is goad him into action.

She felt safe knowing that Nick and Dustin were there for her, especially Nick. Before he left her parents' home in the darkest hours of the morning – just a few hours ago – he'd pulled Raya aside to speak with her privately. She could still feel the warmth of the paper-thin space between them as she leaned against the trunk of the old magnolia tree. He'd only brushed his fingertips across her forehead but that one touch, combined with the intensity of his eyes burning through to her soul, said more than the words that came next.

"Raya, I had you put my cell phone number on your speed dial earlier for a reason. Keep your phone charged and on you at all times. Hit that speed dial button if anything – and I mean anything at all – seems odd or dangerous. I've got your back, but I need you to be careful, and I need you to keep me in the loop. I don't know what it is about you, but you matter to me, so please don't do anything crazy."

Trust didn't come easily to Raya, but in the past few days, she'd let several complete strangers into her confidence. Once her mask had been lifted, she found it easier to allow others into her world. Already, Doc had become like family, quirky Dustin was quickly becoming a friend, and Nick … well, Nick was special. She didn't want to put a label on that relationship just yet, but she didn't hesitate to reassure him.

"I'll keep my phone with me at all times, and I'll also keep my spare battery with me, just in case I need it. I really do understand the danger, Nick, so I promise I'll be cautious. I'm not one of those crazy women you see in horror movies that walks alone at night even though she knows a deranged killer has been spotted in the area. I'm smart, careful, and prepared. You just make sure you have your phone with you – and turned on – just in case I do need to call!"

As she sat down to write, she glanced at the door. It was locked. Her phone was next to her, fully charged, and the extra fully-charged battery was in her jeans pocket. Just as an extra precaution, she also had her cast iron skillet on the seat of the chair next to her. I should probably get a real weapon one of these days, she though, but in the meantime, I can swing a mean frying pan! Speaking out loud to herself, she said, "You wanna play games, asshole? Fine with me. We're starting right now." With that declaration, she began to type.

Chapter 46

Nick didn't wait for Dustin to call. By ten a.m. he was up, and by ten-fifty he was knocking on Dustin's door. "Tell me you have good news, Dustin," he said as he sauntered in without waiting for Dustin to even get up from his work table.

"I do have some news, Nick, but I'm not sure if it's good or not. Our psycho killer was extremely careful to not leave traces, but he missed one tiny spec of DNA that got caught between one poster's corner and the tape he used to hang it on the wall. Because of its location, it could only belong to the person who placed the tape on the poster, so I think we can assume that the DNA belongs to the killer. It was so embedded in the poster board that most instruments would have missed it, but Gloria catches everything!"

Nick looked around. "Gloria? Which of your sexy, curvy electronic doodads did you name Gloria?"

"See this little beauty?" Dustin ran his hand across the molecular analysis instrument that had scanned the posters. "She's not just sexy; she's clever and devious, magical and intelligent. When I completed her design, I decided she was glorious, so I've called her Gloria ever since."

"I'm happy you've found your soul mate, Dustin. Now, tell me. What has Gloria done for us lately?"

"She's given us quite a bit of information actually. I can tell you that the monster we are after is not Glen Simoneaux – or anyone directly related to your father, for that matter."

Nick stood motionless, trying to maintain his composure, finally clearing his throat. "Ok. Noted. And Dustin? Thank you."

Dustin slapped his friend on the back, saying, "No problem, man. So, do you want to know who the killer is, or what?"

"Do you know?"

"Well … no. Not exactly. But Gloria has provided us with one great big giant clue."

"Don't make me beat it out of you, Dustin."

"Gloria ran the DNA sample she found through the various state and federal databases of DNA profiles, and she got a near-match hit. Unfortunately, the DNA profile she pulled is from someone who was incarcerated at the time of the Broussard murders – and in fact – is still incarcerated to this day."

"So, that means…"

"That means someone who is very closely related to our matched felon is our guy. The same principle that lets me eliminate your father and his close relatives as suspects allows me to determine that only a close relative of our felon would fit the DNA profile that Gloria found on that poster."

"So, this felon … what's his name, Dustin?"

"Her name, Nick. Her name is Elise Beraud. Dr. Elise Beraud. She was a quack who ran a psychiatric hospital in Mississippi."

"You don't have to explain who she is, Dustin. I know exactly who she is. She ran the institution that my father was in as a boy. Perry told me a little about it recently, and I followed up with a little research of my own. Gotta love the Internet. Anyway, Dr. Beraud was apparently running some crazy experiments on the patients there. Someone eventually blew the whistle on her, so the place was shut down and she was sent to prison. In fact, that's why Daddy was released from the hospital. Some of the patients were transferred to other institutions, but a few were simply released. Mayor Broussard eventually arranged to have Perry and my father sent to St. Felicity to give them a fresh start."

Dustin picked up his keys and walked to the door. "Ok, so the question now is … who are Dr. Beraud's closest relatives? We need to find out if she has any siblings or children. I suppose it's possible she may even have parents who are still alive, so we should check that as well."

"You run that down, Dustin. Use your high tech gizmos to ferret out that information if you can. I'm going to find out where Dr. Beraud is being held. I think I'll schedule an appointment with the shrink."

Dustin raised his eyebrows and smiled. "Just be careful, Nick. Don't let that woman mess with your head."

"She's the one that should worry, Dustin. I'm in no mood for her games."

Chapter 47

His demeanor when he arrived was stiff but not unpleasant. As soon as he settled into his recliner, she quickly poured a beer into his favorite mug, tuned the TV channel to ESPN, and asked him if he would like her to make supper. He merely grunted, shaking his head, in answer, but he didn't seem particularly unhappy or angry.

Now she realized that she had severely underestimated his mood. He had controlled the conversation, asking seemingly innocent questions, reeling her into his net with each answer she gave.

"Did you miss me while I was gone?"

"You know I always miss you." "Do anything special?"

"No, just the usual. Work, come home, work, come home."

"Really? So, you're saying that your daddy, the good reverend, is a liar?"

"What? No! Of course not. Why would you say that?"

"Less than an hour ago, he was telling me about your little 'girl's night out' with Penny, at Fred's On The River. Seems more than one person mentioned your behavior last night when they saw your Daddy this morning. So was your Daddy lying to me, or were you out drinking and dancing and carrying on last night?"

Sandra gasped. She'd chosen to meet Penny at Fred's On The River because it was an hour's drive from St. Felicity. She hadn't seen anyone she'd known there, so she'd never imagined that word would get back to her father about it. Of course, she hadn't done anything really wrong. Just a few drinks, a few laughs, and a little dancing. Still, she'd known he wouldn't like it, so she'd chosen to hide it from him.

"Oh! That. I, um, I forgot about that, right. Of course, you know how I am. You're always saying how forgetful I am. I did meet Penny for a little while. It was no big deal." Sandra reached out to him but before she was close enough to touch him, he shot out of the chair, grabbed her hair with one hand, wrenched her arm behind her back with his other, and shoved her hard into the wall.

"No.Big.Deal? No big deal? You wait until I leave to run around like a common whore, drinking and dancing, and then lie to me about it, and you think it's no big deal?" He wasn't shouting; in fact, his voice was low, almost at a whisper, but not quite. His low growling words frightened her more than shouting ever could.

Whimpering, she said, "No, no, I didn't mean that. I, please, I'm sorry. I'm so sorry. You're hurting me."

Smiling, he let go of her arm and though he let the grip on her hair grow slack, he didn't release it fully. "Hurt you? No, dear, you must be mistaken. After all these years, you know I would never hurt you. But of course, you also know that I will not tolerate living with a whore!" He bellowed the last word, spraying spittle into her face. His eyes narrowed and his lips curled under in anger. He whipped her head back by the hair, and then kicked her legs out from under her. She slammed knees first, onto the hard floor. Bending down, he put his face to hers and whispered. "Move even one inch without me telling you to, and I'll kill you right now. If you do exactly what I say from now on, however, you'll eventually get your life back. Do you understand what I'm saying, Sandra?"

Sobbing hysterically now, Sandra nodded her head.

"What's that? I can't hear you! Answer me. Do you understand what I'm saying?"

"Yes! Yes, I, I understand!"

He stood, remaining close to her, looking down at her. "Let's make sure you do understand. Raise your left arm and point at the ceiling."

Sandra, kneeling and hunched over, her chest rising and falling as she sobbed, raised her left arm, and pointed at the ceiling as he'd directed.

"Good girl, Sandra. Very good. See? That was easy, wasn't it? Now, all you have to do is stay in that position until I tell you otherwise. Don't fucking move a god damned inch. Are we clear on that?"

"Yes." Sandra continued to cry but she struggled to keep her body as still as she could. She couldn't completely stop her chest from heaving with each sob, but she fought to keep the rest of her body in exactly the same position. As the seconds turned to minutes, she brought the crying under control, but her arm was trembling from being held in that upright position for so long. Her knees were hurting as well, but she believed she could handle that if he would only let her put her arm down. Still, she held her position for another few minutes, until the trembling in her arm turned to unbearable pain and extreme weakness. When she knew she could no longer hold it up, she cried out.

"Please, oh please, I can't hold my arm up any longer, please let me drop it! I'll do everything you say, I promise! Please!"

"Oh, why didn't you say anything? Of course, my dear, you can drop your arm. In fact, why don't you go sit at the dining room table and make yourself comfortable?"

Sandra lifted her head in confusion. He was smiling down at her, gazing at her like one would look at a favorite dog. She flinched when he bent towards her, and then relaxed when he helped her stand and guided her to the table. He pulled out a chair for her and gestured for her to sit. She sat and he guided the chair back towards the table. He then walked around the table, pulled out the chair opposite hers, sat down, and rested his arms on the table. "Comfortable, Sandra?"

Lips trembling, she said quietly, "Yes, thank you."

"Excellent. Now, as I said, as long as you do exactly what I tell you, everything will eventually be back to normal. Keep that in mind, dear."

He sat smiling at her for a few moments, and then stood. As he walked out the front door, he said, "Stay there. I'll be back soon."

Chapter 48

The cell phone ringtone was set to its highest volume, startling Raya as she typed the blog post. The caller ID showed Nick's number, so she answered immediately. "Nick, is everything okay? I'm almost finished with the blog post."

"Everything is fine, Raya, but we have news, so don't publish that blog post just yet."

"News? Is it good or bad? Oh, never mind what it is, just tell it to me." Raya's words were tumbling out in a rush.

"It's good news, I think. Dustin recovered some DNA from one of the posters. He's certain it must be from our killer because it was caught under the tape in a way that could only have happened when the killer placed the tape on the poster. While we don't know exactly who he is, we know several things. One: it wasn't my father, or anyone closely related to him."

"Oh Nick, I know you must be relieved to hear that."

"Yes, actually, I am. But there's more. We got a hit on someone in the system who is a very close match to the DNA, meaning it has to be someone closely related to the match. Unfortunately, the person who came up in the system was in prison during the time of the murders and is still there. So, she has an iron-clad alibi, but it shouldn't be too difficult to figure out which of her close relatives is the killer."

"She? The DNA matched a woman in the system?"

"Yes, it did. And that woman, Dr. Elise Beraud, is the same woman who ran the psychiatric institution that my father was in when he was young. So, while he is no longer a suspect, I can start to see a thread that connects him to the case. I plan to pay the Dr. a visit as soon as I find out where she's incarcerated. She may not be the killer, but she's involved in this, and I aim to find out how. Dustin is working to find out who her siblings, children, and parents might be. I'm going to fill my uncle in on the details as well. While I'm visiting the crazy doctor, I'll be unable to back you up, so I plan to let Uncle Perry take my place as your go-to man. He's the only person I trust to be capable of protecting you if you run into any kind of trouble. I'll arrange for him to come to your place in a few minutes. You two need to meet, swap phone numbers, and get comfortable with each other. When he knocks, make him identify himself before opening the door, got it?"

"Got it! So, what should I do about the blog post?"

"Finish writing it, but don't publish it just yet. I'm hoping to get something out of the doctor that we can use to bait this guy even more. If so, then you can edit the article before publishing, and if I don't get anything we can use, then it will be ready to publish as-is. Does that work for you?"

"Sounds like a good plan. Call me after your visit with Dr. Beraud, Nick."

"As soon as I'm on my way back, I'll call. Remember, Raya. Until I come back, Uncle Perry is the man to call if you need help. Stay safe. I'll see you soon."

After hanging up, Raya spent the next ten minutes writing. When she finished the blog post, she saved it as a draft so it could be edited later if necessary. Okay, now what should I do, she wondered. The knock on the door was her answer.

"Who is it?" she called out.

"Perry Simoneaux. I'll slide some ID under the door. Don't open the door until you have it in your hand."

Raya picked up the card that appeared from under the door and verified that it belonged to a Perry Simoneaux. When she opened the door, she was surprised to see a man that looked like an older version of Nick. He had the look of a man who had lost his charm somewhere in his past, but his face possessed the same handsome features as his nephew's … with a few years tacked on.

Perry didn't wait for an invitation to enter. He quickly moved into the room, closed the door and locked it. He paused for only a moment to introduce himself and shake Raya's hand before moving through each room of her apartment. "Your apartment is as secure as it can be. Don't unlock the windows for any reason. Keep the door locked at all times, and make sure you lock it when you leave, even if you're only walking to the mailbox, so take your keys with you every time you walk out the door."

Raya was still standing near the front door, holding his ID card in her hand. He reached out to take it back and handed her a business card in its place. "My phone number is on the card. Enter it into your phone right now and assign a speed dial number to it. Memorize the speed dial number and memorize my cell phone number too—just in case you lose your phone, you'll know my number by heart. While you're doing that, give me your number, and I'll save it in my phone's address book as well."

Despite Raya's natural tendency to bristle when someone else tried to take control, she admired Perry's gruff, no-nonsense handling of the situation. She could see why Nick would trust him to protect her. After memorizing Perry's number, he quizzed her repeatedly until he was sure that she wouldn't forget it.

"So now what do we do?" Raya asked.

"We wait to hear from Nick. If you don't mind, I'd like to stay here with you for an hour or so. If I'm going to be responsible for your welfare, I'd like to get to know you a little. The better I know you, the more likely I'll know where to find you if I need to track you down. So, let's start with what you do in a typical day."

The two sat on the couch, drinking tea that Raya brewed earlier. She filled Perry in on the mundane details of her life, including the stores she frequented, the restaurants and fast food chains she ate at most often, the gas stations she used, and the location of her nearest bank branch. She tried to leave nothing of any importance out. By the time she finished, Perry even knew the types of doughnuts she favored—jelly-filled—and the days of the week she shopped for groceries.

Raya sat back and grinned. "Now that you know everything about me, would you mind if I asked you to give me a little insider information on Nick? Something only his uncle would tell a girl?"

That finally got a small smile out of Perry. "I don't know how much he'd appreciate me telling tales, so I think I'll stick to sharing just one small bit of information that shouldn't get me into too much trouble with him."

"I'll take whatever tidbits you care to share, Mr. Simoneaux."

"Just call me Perry, Raya. Now, Nick, he's always been a popular young man, but he's never had a roommate. He still lives alone, although don't tell Mimi I said that."

"Mimi? Who is that?" she asked.

"Mimi is the Blue Catahoula Cur that I gave him when she was just a pup."

"Oh, I love Catahoulas—the Louisiana Leopard dog! They are so pretty, with those amazing crackled glass blue eyes and leopard-like coat."

"Yep, and Mimi is the finest example of a Catahoula I've ever seen. She's not only beautiful, but she's smart and sweet too. She pretty much rules the house, you know, and she hates being referred to as a dog. Don't look at me like that, Raya. I'm telling you, she's smart enough to know what's being said about her. Nick and I both consider her to be a member of the family, and she's certainly got a bigger heart than any person I know. I tried explaining to her once that being a dog meant that she was superior to humans, but she gave me a 'look', so I never mentioned it again. She may not appreciate being classified as a dog, but as far as I'm concerned, that's the highest compliment I can give."

"I understand, Perry. Dogs do have the biggest hearts. Is she a hunting dog?"

"Hardly! Catahoulas are natural hunting dogs, but Mimi made it quite clear to me early on that she had no intention of traipsing around through the woods. She would sit down and not budge. In fact, that's why I gave her to Nick, since he isn't a hunter. I can only assume she's a city girl, and merely tolerates the fact that we live in a small town.

Anyway, Nick and Mimi share a fairly large house. He bought it from one of old man Henshaw's sons a few years ago. It needed a lot of work, but over time, Nick has brought it back to its original beauty. The back yard extends all the way to the river. If you're ever having a hard time finding Nick, hop onto one of the four-wheelers he has parked in the back, and follow the trail down to the river. You're almost guaranteed to find him there, toes dangling in the water, fishing pole in hand. And that's all the information you're going to get out of me today."

"Thanks, Perry. That's actually enough information to give me a lot of insight into him. But don't worry, I won't let on that you shared any secrets."

Chapter 49

According to the records that Dan pulled for Nick, Elise Beraud's medical license was stripped from her nearly 30 years ago, just before her incarceration. She was sent to the only Mississippi prison that housed female prisoners, and was still there today, serving a 40 year sentence. Located near Jackson, it was a three hour drive, so Nick would have to leave soon. They allowed some flexibility in visitation schedules for law enforcement officers, but he still had to meet the expanded deadline or wait until the next day.

"Dan, were you able to dig up any photos of Ms. Beraud?"

"Yep, got 'em right here. Shame such a lady had to waste away in a women's prison all these years."

Nick raised his eyebrows at that but understood the meaning once he saw the photos. The top picture was the mug shot taken the day of her arrest, 9 years before the Broussard murders. A mug shot usually makes a driver's license photo look like a studio portrait, but this mug shot could have graced the cover of a fashion magazine—minus the fashion.

Despite the serious facial expression, Elise's full, perfectly-formed lips curved upwards slightly at the corners. Her small well-shaped nose was set off by large brown eyes. Long dark hair created a natural frame for softly sculpted cheekbones, and a slight dimple rested naturally in her chin. The result was a strangely compelling mix of beauty, class, elegance, and sensuality, with a touch of girl-next-door innocence. Even in prison scrubs, she would turn heads on the street - although she might never walk a public street again.

Nick flipped through the rest of the photos. Most were grainy surveillance shots taken before her arrest. In some, she wore a long, white doctor's coat, and in others, she was dressed in evening wear. Regardless of the quality of the photo, or the clothing she wore, in each photograph, she maintained the same allure. She was the kind of woman that men would fall in love with on sight, and although Nick wasn't sure how women normally reacted to other women, he suspected that they would rush to be her new best friend. Nothing about this woman even hinted at the possibility that a cold, cruel, sinister soul lay underneath such a warm, inviting form.

There were no recent photos, but he quickly did the math in his head. She would be 69 years old now. He wondered if her dark interior would be visible now that her youthful beauty had withered. No point in wondering or wasting any more time, he thought. Time to go see this evil beauty for myself.

"Thanks for compiling this so quickly, Dan. The next beer is on me. See you tomorrow."

Nick left, driving northeast along winding back roads towards I-55, unaware that tomorrow might never come.

Chapter 50

He hadn't felt this alive in twenty years. He would research his players tomorrow, but today was reserved for practice. Those few glorious moments when he'd kept Sandra kneeling on the floor in front of him had nearly overwhelmed him. That "special lust" he'd suppressed for so long came bursting forth, begging to be set free. He'd managed to contain it but only barely. He'd had to leave for a short time, to regroup, to take control over the beast within, to set a pace that would make this practice game last as long as possible.

He was confident she would still be sitting at the table where he'd ordered her to stay. Over the years, he'd slowly turned her into an obedient serf. He allowed her to assert her independence occasionally because such rebellion gave her false confidence. As long as she believed she maintained some element of control, she would never let others know what their lives behind closed doors were really like. And of course, each time she rebelled, she gave him one more reason to add to the list of actions which he could use against her in the future. Today, her future had arrived.

He smiled as he opened the door and saw her sitting demurely at the table, eyes down, rivers of makeup staining her cheeks. When he placed the brightly wrapped gift on the table in front of her, she jumped as though she expected him to give her a snake. She looked up at him in surprise but said nothing.

"Go ahead, darling, open it." He kissed the top of her head, walked to the other side of the table, and sat down opposite her once again. She fumbled with the ribbon and gift wrap, her hands still shaking, but she finally revealed the gift inside.

"What is this?" she asked.

"What does it look like?" he replied.

"Well, it sorta looks like a dice, but it's in the shape of a pyramid, and it has letters on it."

"It not only 'sorta' looks like a dice, it is one, although technically speaking, since you are holding only one, the proper name is 'die', not 'dice'. Nevertheless, in this world of text messages and Facebook statuses, using the word 'dice' will suffice."

She studied it, her brows furrowed, then looked back up at him, confused once again. "Th-thank you," she said softly.

"I'm sorry but unless I'm mistaken, you sound less than thankful."

"No, no, I mean, yes, I mean..." Tears rolled down her face again. She struggled to speak coherently. "Thank you very much. It's ... lovely." She smiled through the tears, making him think of that old song, Tears of A Clown. Who sang that? he wondered. Oh right, Smokey Robinson and The Miracles. He began to hum the tune aloud, delighted to be adding to her confusion even more. He could feel the heat rise in his groin, and though he fought the urge, he knew he would be unable to resist for much longer. As much as he wanted to make the game last—he wished it would last longer than it had that day twenty years ago—he knew he was quickly losing control. It was time to move the game forward more quickly, before he found himself at the end of the game before it was officially over.

Abruptly, he stopped humming the song. He slammed his fists on the table and shot out of the chair, lifting the table up a few inches as his hips flew upward. Sandra shrieked and watched in horror as the dice careened out of her hand, bounced off the table, then rolled awkwardly across the floor, finally coming to a stop under the couch. She instinctively cowered, arms covering her head, when she saw him rush around the table.

Satisfied that he had her in exactly the state he wanted, he sped past her to retrieve the dice from its hiding place. She was still hunched over when he approached her from behind. He leaned across her back, reached over her shoulder, and placed the dice on the table in front of her. The feel of her trembling back against his chest caused his erection to strain against his fly. Her fear was his aphrodisiac; her obedience was his justification.

Still leaning over her back, his breath blowing her hair, he whispered in her ear. "Let's try this again, shall we? Here, darling. I have a present for you. Do you like it?" Before she could reply, he wrapped his hand around her throat, squeezing just enough to keep her silenced. He continued whispering, his lips brushing against her earlobe. "Pick up the dice and look at it." When she obeyed, he said, "As you can see, in this game, you always have a choice. On this side of the dice is Choice A. On that side is Choice B. And there's always the option of choosing X. Let's see how simple the game really is. I asked you a question. Do you like your present? You can choose A—YES or B—NO. Do you understand how to play?"

Sandra nodded her head. "Good! Do you have any questions?"

"What is the X for?" Her voice was so low he could barely hear her, but of course, he didn't need to hear. He already knew the question would be asked. That's what made him such a great master of the game.

"Don't worry about the X for now, my dear. We'll discuss that part of the game when necessary. For now, all you have to do is place the dice so that your answer is facing me. Do you like your present? Remember, A is for Yes and B is for No."

Without even a moment's hesitation, she quickly faced the side with the letter 'A' engraved on it towards them both.

"You do? You like it?" He stood and back away from her, clasping his hands together in glee. "I'm so glad you like it! I knew you would! I know you so well, don't I? After all these years, I can still pick just the right present for my girl." Willing his lust to hold steady, he returned to his seat opposite Sandra. "Round two. Do you ever smoke cigarettes? If yes, choose A. If no, choose B."

Her eyes, though nearly swollen shut from crying, opened wide and looked around, searching the room for help or escape; her head reared back as though struck.

He narrowed his eyes to slits and growled. "Answer the question, bitch."

Slowly, she turned the dice, leaving side B facing him. His slap spun her head to the side with so much force, she nearly fell off the chair. She remained doubled over, holding her hand over her burning cheek, never noticing he had come around the table until he was at her side. He wrapped her hair around his fist and yanked her upright in her chair. The sensation he'd first felt when he had grasped her hair earlier while forcing her to kneel on the floor rushed through him again. It took every ounce of self-control to keep from shoving her head between his legs. Instead, he slammed her forehead into the table, again, and again, and again. He thought he could hear her screaming, but the pounding in his head was like the roar of a lion. Just as the lion was ready to rip her throat out, he felt her going slack in his hands. He jerked his fist free of her hair, cupped her chin in his hands, and looked into her eyes. "Stay with me, Sandra, stay with me. See? I've stopped. It's okay. Stay with me."

A lump was already forming on her forehead, but she was conscious. He knew her eyes would blacken later, but he wasn't concerned about that. No one would ever see them. No one would ever see her again. He left her sitting there, dazed. Now that he'd retained mastery over his lust, he returned to his seat. He noticed a thick wad of her hair still caught in his hand. It gave him pleasure to think of how it must have hurt when each strand was ripped out of her scalp, so he allowed the threads to remain snaked around his fingers while he resumed game play.

Chapter 51

Nick assumed that Dustin would start his research into Elise Beraud's family ties by tapping into the various federal or state law enforcement databases. Dustin knew, however, that some data was more easily obtained from the public databases. In this case, he turned to ancestry.com, which had an enormous amount of information compiled about the world's families. Many people have no idea how easy it is to trace a family tree these days. Most of the work has already been done by others before them.

He renewed his "World Explorer" subscription every six months, which enabled him to always have access to every record within ancestry.com's vast database. Within minutes of logging in, Dustin had a list of Elise's closest relatives. Of course, it was possible that some records were missing, but as long as he had a list to start from, filling in any missing gaps should be relatively easy.

Since both of Elise's parents and one of her siblings had died years earlier, Dustin was left with a short list of only three possible familial DNA matches.

Elise Favrot Beraud, wife of Pierre Beraud, had one brother who might still be alive; Andre Favrot. Ancestry.com had no record of his death, but death records were often missing. Since Andre would be 83 years old now, there was a good chance that he was not the man he was looking for. It was possible, of course, for such an elderly man to still be playing such a deadly game, but Dustin decided to go with his gut on this one.

I won't ignore you, Andre, but you're going on the bottom of the list for now, he thought. I have a feeling we're hunting someone who still has an agile body and a sharp mind.

Elise's baby sister, Janice, was young enough to peak Dustin's interest. Normally he would put women at the bottom of a list of serial killer suspects, but since Elise herself had proved to be capable of heinous experiments on already weak and tortured souls, he was more willing to consider her female sibling as a potential murderess.

He entered the only information he had about her— name and birth date—into CRAP, the custom search engine he had developed and honed over the years. It could search all federal, state, and local law enforcement databases, as well as many of the world's databases for which he did not have official clearance to access.

When asked about the program's name, he explained that CRAP stood for Criminal Records Archive Probe, but in reality, he'd named it CRAP because the criminals he sought were always found swimming in the cesspool of humanity. He enjoyed pretending that it had never even occurred to him that the acronym he'd given his search engine would be the butt of its own joke.

While he let CRAP conduct its search, he moved on to the next name on the list, Etienne Beraud. Etienne was Elise and Pierre's only child. Like his Aunt Janice, only his birth date was available from ancestry.com, with no reference to his current marital status or place of residence. At the time of the Broussard murders, Etienne would have been a young man, making him middle-aged now. As far as Dustin was concerned, that put Mr. Beraud at the top of the list.

Dustin opened a second search window and entered Etienne's data into CRAP as well. Both searches finished processing within seconds of each other, and both returned the same message. "No results. Broaden the search?"

You aren't going to make this easy for me, are you? he thought. He clicked the BROADEN SEARCH button for both Janice and Etienne. This would instruct CRAP to reach into as many public and private databases as possible to dig up any information on his prime suspects.

A broad search would take considerably longer and would often yield quite a few "false positives"—records that belonged to other people who happened to have the same or similar names. The results would be less precise, and would take more manual effort to comb through, but it would still make the task far easier, and would shave off days of time he would otherwise have had to spend if he'd used the standard law enforcement search engines.

He dialed Nick's number but was sent immediately to voice mail. "Nick, I have possible familial DNA matches for Elise Beraud. I don't have enough information yet to narrow it down further, but I should know something more within the next few hours. Call me later."

Chapter 52

"Left thumb or right thumb, Sandra? Choose A for left or B for right."

"No! Please, no, I can't." She was no longer crying, having gotten past that point after she'd had to choose between cutting a small triangular shape on her forehead or shaving her head. She'd chosen B, shaving her head, knowing it would grow back eventually. Afterwards, he'd forced her to look into a mirror while he taunted her and peppered her with ridicule for nearly an hour. Eventually, the tears stopped flowing, and even now, with a new choice before her, only dry panic remained.

"You get one more chance to choose, Sandra. A for left thumb; B for right thumb. Which will it be?"

"Neither. Neither!" she screamed.

He slammed her left hand onto the table, holding it there with his own left hand while she struggled to escape his grasp. With his right hand, he swung the blade down quickly, slicing off her thumb with one clean motion. Before her screams had faded, he'd sliced her right thumb off, though not as cleanly as the first.

He'd expected her to faint, but instead she sat there screaming, her hands still lying flat against the tabletop, each thumb positioned about a half inch away from her hand. While she screamed, he took the time to turn up the volume on the concerto that was already blasting from the speakers. Then, with careful tenderness, he bandaged her hands to curb the bleeding.

When her screams finally turned to moans, he sat across from her and said, "Now you know what the third side of the dice is for. X is the choice I will make if you refuse to choose either A or B." He then took each of her thumbs and placed them, one over the other, in the formation of an X in front of him. "Do you understand, Sandra?" This was the point at which she passed out—for the first time that day.

Chapter 53

Nick tried to hide his surprise when he walked into the interview room. He'd imagined a withered old crone would greet him with a witches cackle, but instead he met a still-attractive older woman whose graceful demeanor felt all wrong in this nearly-bare yet very grungy room.

He quickly decided to take a different approach with her than he'd planned. He would play the charmed—and charming—innocent young cop, letting her believe she had the upper hand over him.

"Ms. Beraud, I am Detective Nick Simoneaux, but I prefer to be called just Nick."

"Well, then, Just Nick, it's a pleasure to meet you." Elise's smile matched her eyes, both crinkling with amusement.

Nick returned her smile. "You can leave out the 'Just', if that's all right with you, Ms. Beraud."

"Please call me Elise. We are on a first name basis now, aren't we, Nick?"

Her voice had a silky tone that felt like a caress; each word she spoke lightly brushing against his skin, though the two of them were eight feet apart. He could already see how she had effectively controlled the patients that she'd abused in the psychiatric institution. Even at this age, her looks and voice had a persuasive quality that could sway the staunchest foe. He could only imagine how much more powerful she'd been twenty-nine years earlier, just before she'd finally been seen for what she really was.

"Yes, Elise, first names it is from now on. I hope you're well. While we chat, please feel free to let me know if you need anything. I'm here because I was hoping I could get your help, so I'm happy to ensure your comfort during our conversation. Perhaps I can arrange for you to have something that isn't normally allowed. A special soft drink? A smoke?"

"That's very kind of you, Nick. I don't smoke, and I've never been fond of sodas. However, for twenty-nine years, I've been craving a hot, strong cup of dark roast Community coffee, the brand that Louisiana made famous." She tilted her head, closed her eyes, and continued. "Even though I grew up in Mississippi, I always insisted on serving Community coffee. Now, each morning, just before I'm fully awake, I imagine I can smell it brewing, that pungent odor drifting into my dreams. Is there any chance you could make that dream come true?"

"I'm certain I can make that happen. If you don't mind, I'll step out for a minute to arrange that." Nick exited and joined the warden in the observation room.

Warden Sully chuckled when Nick entered the room. "Don't tell me she's already charmed you, Detective? Surely you're not so easily swayed as that."

Nick smiled. "No, Warden, I'm in full control of both the situation and my senses, I assure you. I thought I'd try to entice the bear with a little honey first, or in this case sweet talk and coffee, but if that doesn't work, I'll turn off the charm and bring out the wolf. So, what do you say? Do you think I can get that cup of hot Community coffee for our she-bear in there?"

"It's already on order. I phoned it into my private chef the second you agreed to the lady's request. It will be here in a few minutes. I ordered a cup for you as well. Unwrapped sugar cubes and loose, powdered cream will be provided also. I recommend that you stand as far away from the prisoner as possible, so she has no chance of throwing hot coffee in your face."

"Noted, and thank you," Nick said.

"Detective, this is the first time I've had the chance to get a glimpse inside that lunatic's head. She's never agreed to speak with anyone before, so I'm happy to oblige. Take as much time as you'd like with her. I know the rules say that you only have until 6:00 p.m. before we lock it down, but I'll make an exception in this case. I've freed up my entire evening to watch this match between the two of you. So, get back in there, and entertain me, Detective."

"I'll do my best, sir."

When he returned to the interrogation room, Elise beamed at him as though she were greeting an old friend. He returned the smile and said, "You and I will be drinking Community coffee together shortly, Elise."

"Thank you, Nick. That's very kind of you. Now do tell me, what can I possibly do to help you?" Elise asked.

"I believe your special … talents … and knowledge of how the mind works could help me in an investigation. In essence, I would appreciate it if you would act as a sort of 'consultant' to me as I attempt to understand the particular mindset and psyche of a criminal who has evaded capture for a long time. Would you be willing to share your expertise with me, Elise?" Nick gave Elise his classic "pretty please" look. He'd developed the look when he was five but had perfected it by the time he was seven years old. His head tilted slightly to the right, eyebrows raised just a little, he looked sideways at the person he hoped to persuade and blinked. Southern women often called this look, "making sweet eyes".

Before Elise could answer, two throwaway cups of steaming coffee were delivered. Nick stood and walked to the corner of the room farthest from Elise. He leaned against the wall and took a sip, while watching Elise make a production out of adding sugar and cream to hers. She stirred with her finger, then grasping the cup in both hands, she leaned back in the chair, brought the cup to her face, and breathed in the scent she'd dreamed of for so long. Finally, she put her lips to the cup and took a long, lingering sip. Each movement was slow, graceful, and naturally sensual. Nick could almost feel the liquid sliding down her throat as he watched her react to the taste. She looked up at Nick after that first taste, her eyes shimmering with the hint of tears.

"Thank you, Nick. I'll help you in any way I can."

She had the crazy knack of being able to make him feel as though he should be grateful to her. Instead of answering right away, he took another sip of coffee and remained quiet. This gave him the time to compose himself and remember that he was here to mess with her head, not the other way around.

Nick decided he wouldn't ease into this but would start off with a killer question. "Elise, in your professional psychiatric opinion, does a mental patient have the capacity to plan and execute an elaborate game that results in the torture and murder of several people, all without leaving behind a trace of evidence?"

He noticed that she had no visible reaction to the question at all. She gently placed the paper cup on the table, but kept both hands cradled around it, as though she were absorbing the warmth from it.

"Certainly. One could probably make the case that most such criminals should have the 'mental patient' label applied to them. Of course, as it is with all things, the real answer lies in the realm of 'it depends'. Are all mental patients capable of executing a complex plan without getting caught? No, definitely not. But are some capable? Absolutely."

He knew she expected him to continue questioning her, but he preferred to make her wait. He kept his eyes locked with hers, probing her thoughts and letting the silence become heavy between them.

"I see. So, we wouldn't be out of line to consider someone who has been released from an institution to be a potential suspect. You'll have to forgive my complete lack of knowledge in this area, but I was wondering… What makes people crazy? Does it really all stem from the mother, like they say?"

Nick hoped this would question would spark some emotion, and he wasn't disappointed.

"We don't use the word 'crazy' to describe mental illness." Her words were no longer silky smooth. Instead, she spoke in a harsh, clipped manner. "And no, the mother is not always to blame."

Just as quickly as the words erupted from her, she shifted back into her softer, more persuasive voice. "Of course, parents play a large role in our lives, so it's natural that many children from abusive homes will grow up to have psychological issues. It's certainly not uncommon for some of these patients to have unhealthy relationships with their mothers, but that is only one of many possible causes." He was impressed that none of the clipped tones remained in her voice. She'd disposed of that burst of anger nearly instantly. He worried that she would be a tough nut to crack, but he was determined to pull information out of her before the day was over.

"Thank you for clearing that up for me, Elise. I guess I shouldn't believe everything I hear, huh?" He gave her one of his most endearing smiles; the one that all the elderly women mentioned when they tried to convince their granddaughters that he would be perfect for them. "Would you like more coffee?"

"Yes, thank you." He poured the remainder of the coffee that had been delivered in a thermos into her cup, and then retreated quickly back to his corner of the room.

"Ok, so here's another question I have, Elise. Let's consider this scenario. Is it possible or even likely that siblings might both be mentally unstable; or even that a parent's mental illness might be passed on to the children? Could sons and daughters turn out to be just as crazy and evil as the parent?"

Elise's eyes narrowed and her graceful demeanor collapsed. Nick hoped he'd broken through her polished false exterior.

Chapter 54

Raya was going stir-crazy. After dusting twice, rearranging the knick-knacks in the living room, and staring at the phone every other minute, she decided enough was enough. Once again, that monster is controlling me, she thought. Dammit, I said I wouldn't let him do that to me, but here I am, hiding in my apartment, instead of living my life. I know Nick wants me here, but I can't take this any longer. I'll call Perry and tell him my plans. That way, he can cover my back just like he promised Nick he'd do.

She dialed Perry's number expecting to get his voice mail, but he picked up on the first ring.

"Raya? Anything wrong?" he asked, with obvious concern in his voice.

"Nothing some fresh air won't fix," she replied. "I'm going to the Farmer's Market to pick up some fruit and veggies for dinner tonight, and then I plan to go visit Mom and Dad for a while. I just wanted to let you know where I'll be, so no one panics."

"Wait till I get there, and I'll follow you, Raya."

"I can't sit here another minute, Perry. Look, the hotel you're staying at isn't very far from the Farmer's Market. You'll be there before I will, so I'll just meet you there. Then you can follow me to my parents' house from there if you'd like."

"I'm not crazy about you walking out your door alone for even a moment, but if you promise you'll be on alert the second you open the door, and you'll get into your car and drive away quickly, I'll agree to the plan."

Raya almost felt sorry for putting Perry in the position of having to worry so much about her, but she was determined to live her life fully now. She had no plans to be foolish. She did make sure no one was around when she opened the front door. She did walk quickly to her car, unlocking it remotely so she could jump in and leave immediately. She even kept an eye on the cars in her rear view mirror as she drove, just in case someone might have followed her. By the time she reached the market, she was confident that there was nothing to fear. No one had followed her, and she saw Perry waiting in the parking lot. Everything was fine.

She and Perry spent the next half hour getting to know one another better. Despite Sue's earlier warning that Perry was an old sourpuss, Raya found him sweet and charming.

He made grumbling noises a few times, in protest of her insistence on searching through all of the produce in the bins for the best of the bunch. But his grumbling was obviously his way of playing the part that was expected of him. When he wasn't pretending to be a curmudgeon, he was entertaining her with stories of Nick's childhood. By the time the two of them had filled her trunk with bags of produce, they were laughing together like old friends.

"Perry, just follow me. My parents' house isn't far." Raya made sure Perry pulled out of the parking lot behind her, but by the time she'd made the first turn off the market road, her thoughts had drifted to the stories Perry had told of Nick's boyhood pranks. She was chuckling out loud as she pulled into her parents' driveway. It was only after she'd stepped out of the car that she realized Perry was nowhere in sight.

"Crap!" she said aloud. She looked up and down the street but didn't see any sign of Perry's car, so she dialed his cell. This time she expected him to answer right away, but instead, she reached his voice mail. "Perry, I'm so sorry, I didn't notice that I lost you along the way. Just give me a call and I'll direct you to here from wherever you are." She hung up, thinking her phone would ring right away, but it stayed silent. Frowning, Raya decided to go inside and wait for his call there.

Just as she started to insert her key into their door's lock, she noticed the door wasn't completely closed. She pushed it open and yelled, "Mom! Dad! Anybody here?"

The silence that answered her made her nervous, but she had no intention of panicking until she looked out back. She crossed the living room, walked out the back door, and saw that no one was in the back yard. Retracing her steps, she went back out to the front, and lifted the old garage door that her father had been promising to replace for years. Both cars, her mother's old Camry and her father's Jeep Cherokee were side by side in the garage. Maybe they're taking a nap, she thought. I'll go back in and check the rest of the house.

Five minutes later, after searching the same rooms over and over again, Raya was more than concerned. Her mother's purse was on the kitchen counter and Raya knew that she never went anywhere without her purse. She'd tried reaching Perry several times, but he still hadn't answered the phone.

"You idiot!" Raya said aloud to herself. "I'll just call Mom's cell and find out where they are. Maybe they just walked over to a neighbor's house." She pulled up her mother's name in her phone's address book and pressed the Call button. The ringing sound that came from her mother's purse brought her fully to the edge of panic.

Chapter 55

Dustin left another message for Nick, when he still couldn't reach him. "Nick, I've narrowed our suspect list down to just one person. I was able to eliminate Elise's siblings. Her brother was injured in the Korean War and has been severely handicapped and in a wheelchair ever since. It took a little more digging, but I was finally able to track down Elise's sister. She's been living and working as a missionary in South America for the past thirty years. That leaves only one person who could possibly be a familial DNA match— Elise's son—Etienne Beraud. Etienne would have been 27 at the time of the Broussard murders, but he moved out of his mother's home when he was 18 or so, which was sometime before his mother was incarcerated and your father was released from the institution. That's where the trail goes cold. I don't know where he went, and I haven't been able to find any records for him after that. He just vanished. But you and I know that rarely happens by accident. My guess is that the evil doctor's son changed his identity, so tracking him down won't be as easy as I'd like. Don't worry though. We'll find him. I'll call you if I learn more."

Just as Dustin pressed the End Call button, his cell vibrated and began playing Disney's 'It's A Small World'—the ringtone Dustin chose because it rated so high on the annoyance scale. The number shown on-screen was one he didn't recognize so he decided to let voicemail grab it. He'd check it later, but right now, he wanted to touch base with someone who might know more about Etienne. He hadn't spoken to her in a while, and she might not be receptive to getting a call from him now, but it was worth a try. He still had her in his phone contacts even though she'd once told him to forget she ever existed. No matter how much time went by, he'd never been able to press the Delete option next to her name. Taking a deep breath, he pressed the Call button.

"What?!"

Dustin smiled despite the harsh welcome on the other end of the phone. Hey, he figured, at least she'd answered even though she knew it was me calling. That's a positive sign, right?

"Hi, Sharon. This really is a life-or-death kind of call – not mine, by the way – so please hear me out. People's lives really are at stake." Dustin had to look at his phone's screen to make sure the call was still connected because there was nothing but a long, steady silence emanating from it.

"Ok, Dustin, I'll hear you out, but I swear, if this isn't urgent, I swear, I'll … I'll … well, I don't know what I'll do, but I'll definitely be pissed! So. Whose lives are at stake and how am I involved?"

Dustin tried not to let his smile show through in his voice, but inside, he was doing a little celebratory dance. Maybe there was hope after all. For now, though, he kept those thoughts to himself. "I'm working with Nick on a case," he began.

"Nick! I should have known. What scrape have you two gotten yourselves into this time?"

He could almost see the cartoon steam coming from her ears, curling around those auburn curls he used to love to pull. The way they bounced back like a spring always fascinated him, especially when she was lying on top of him, her hair hanging in his face.

"No scrapes, darlin'."

"Don't call me darlin'!"

"Sorry. Sharon. Anyway, this isn't one of our old Nick and Dustin escapades. Nick's working a bonafide whacko-murder case—a big one—and we know who we're looking for, but we've run into a brick wall in our search for him. As fate would have it, the sick bastard comes from your area of the country, so I thought you might be able to help us locate him. Honestly, I wouldn't be bothering you if it wasn't really important. This guy has at least three more people he's targeting, and if we don't find him fast, we may not stop him in time. So, is there any chance we can take a break from your hatred of me just long enough to work together on this? I promise you can go back to despising me once this is all over."

Her sigh was deep and audible. "Fine. Whatever, Dustin. I happen to be in your neck of the woods this week anyway, so maybe it is Fate intervening. I'll have to have a long talk with Lady Fate about her interference later, but okay, for now, I'll pretend you aren't the face I throw darts at every night. I'm heading to a late-afternoon meeting right now, so I can't get this over and done with right now, on the phone. After the meeting, I'll be dining at George's, next to Regal Hotel, where I'm staying. I have reservations at seven. Since I'm not fond of dining alone, feel free to meet me there for dinner. If you aren't there by seven-thirty, don't bother showing up. I don't plan to wait around for you ever again."

"You won't have to wait on me, I promise. See you at seven. And Sharon? Thank you." Dustin hoped he could send Lady Fate a silent thank you later, if he could manage to break through even a little of Sharon's icy reserve tonight.

He put the phone down and noticed the voicemail icon blinking. He'd already forgotten about the earlier call he'd ignored, so he was glad for the reminder. Technology would always be one of Dustin's best friends.

"You have one new voicemail," the robotic woman's voice said. "Press 1 to listen to it now." Dustin pressed the button dutifully.

"Dustin, this is Raya. Something's happened! Or at least, I think something has happened! I don't know what to think!"

Dustin could hear the panic in her voice.

"I'm at my parents' house. They aren't here, but the door was open, and their cars are here, and so is my mother's purse and cell phone. Something's wrong. I think they may be missing! And I lost Perry and he's not answering, and I don't know what to do! Nick's not answering, you're not answering. What the hell is going on? Somebody help! Call me!"

"Son of a bitch," Dustin muttered, ending the voice mail call and hitting the Return Call button quickly. "Answer, Raya, answer!" he whispered aloud.

"Hello?" Raya's voice didn't sound any less panicky than it had on the voicemail.

"Raya, it's Dustin. I just got your message. What's going on?"

"Oh Dustin, I don't know what to do!" Raya explained about her trip to the Farmer's Market, Perry's disappearance, and her fears that her parents might be in real trouble.

Dustin's mind was reeling. Raya was an hour away from him, in Lafayette. Sharon would be expecting him at George's in an hour and a half. He couldn't be in both places at once. Nick was even farther away, in Mississippi, and he'd been unreachable for hours anyway.

"Raya, have you tried getting in touch with Doc Forester? He lives near there, right?"

"No, I haven't! I don't know why I didn't think to call Doc."

"Ok, here's what I want you to do, Raya. Get in your car and leave your parents' house immediately. Call Dr. Forester after you've driven away from the house. If you can get in touch with him, arrange to meet him either at his home or office. Then immediately call me back. Don't wait to call me. If I don't hear from you in five minutes, I'm going to imagine all sorts of things, so call me back right after you call the doc, okay?"

"Okay, Dustin. I'm in the car and leaving now. Talk to you soon."

For the next two minutes, Dustin quickly devised a plan and was ready by the time 'It's A Small World' started playing again.

"Dustin, I spoke with Doc. I'm meeting him at his office. I'll be there in just a minute."

Relief washed over Dustin. "Great, that's good news, Raya. Now here's what I think you should do next. Try to get Dr. Forester to go with you, but even if he can't, I want you to come here. You need to be in a place where you are safe. I'll arrange for a place for you to stay, but I don't want to discuss where over the phone. Just head in this direction and call me just before you get to town. I'll tell you where to meet me then."

"But I can't just leave here, with my parents missing and Perry out there somewhere!" Raya was obviously prepared to put up a fight, but Dustin knew there wasn't time for a long drawn-out compromise.

"Raya, please trust me. You can't help your parents or Perry as long as you are in danger yourself. We will find them all, but you need to get out of there until we can all coordinate a search. Oh, and please ask Dr. Forester to drive. You're in no shape to be behind the wheel for long. Can I count on you to just trust me, Raya?"

For the second time in the last fifteen minutes, Dustin heard a woman's deep sigh come through his phone. I might need to work on my phone etiquette, he thought.

"Okay, Dustin. I'm pulling into Doc's office parking lot now. I'll see if he'll come with me, and if so, I'll let him drive. You're right, by the way. I really shouldn't be driving right now. I'm shaking like a leaf. But if he can't come, I'll pull myself together enough to drive safely."

"Thank you, Raya. Remember, call me in an hour, and I'll have a place arranged for you to stay by then. Be careful and try not to worry too much. We'll find them."

As Dustin hung up the phone, he wondered how Sharon would react when he told her she was going to have two strangers sharing her hotel room tonight. If she refused, he would arrange a separate room for Raya and Doc, but he would be much happier knowing that Sharon was with them. Other than Nick, Sharon was the only other person he would trust as a bodyguard. He'd seen both her gun and martial arts skills in action. Raya and Dr. Forester would be safe with her. All he'd have to do is convince her to let them move into her hotel room tonight. On the other hand, I imagine Sharon would rather share her room with two total strangers than with me, he thought.

Chapter 56

Doc didn't hesitate. Before Raya could finish asking if he would drive east with her, he was already bustling her towards his car. "I know most of your parents' friends and co-workers, Raya. I'll call them all while we're on the road."

"Good idea, Doc. And I have an idea or two of my own," Raya said. "None of us have heard from Nick all day either, so I have to assume that he may be missing as well. If that's the case, then I can't sit around and wait. I'm going to go ahead and publish the blog post just as we planned last night. Wow, was that really just last night?"

"This morning, actually. I think we all headed home about two a.m., wasn't it?"

"It was, Doc. So much has happened since then." Raya reached into her handbag and pulled out her iPad tablet. A few keystrokes later, and she was logged into her account at the true crime website. She'd already submitted the blog post but had left it in 'draft mode', so she could edit it before publishing it. Now that her parents were missing, though, she needed to publish it immediately. She could only hope that the killer would see it—and respond the way they'd planned.

"Cross your fingers, Doc." Raya clicked the Publish button. "Now, it's time to share it with St. Felicity's biggest gossips." Sue was first on the list of people to tell.

"Hi, Sue, this is Raya. Yes, thanks, I'm fine. Listen, I wanted to tell you that my first blog post about the Broussard murders has just been published. I'll text the web address to you. Do you think you could make sure everyone in town knows about it?"

She knew it wouldn't take long to spread to everyone in town, but she couldn't take chances. She emailed both the local newspaper and radio station, as well. All she could do now was hope that news of the blog post reached the only person that mattered—the killer.

Chapter 57

Dan rang the doorbell a second time, but the music from inside was so loud, he doubted it was heard. Why the hell anybody would listen to that snooty old music was something Officer Guidry would never understand. He wouldn't have guessed he'd hear it being blasted here at this house. He decided to pound the door with his fist, but if no one answered, he was going home. He needed a hot shower and several six-packs to forget the job he'd just had to do.

The third time his fist connected with the door, it was swung open, a hand grabbed his shirt, and he was yanked into the dark foyer of the house. Instinct made Dan cock his arm back, but he stopped when he saw his oppressor's face staring back at him.

"What the hell, man?" Dan shouted. "What's with this loud-ass stupid fucking music?"

"Shut up! The music is none of your concern. Just give me your report."

Dan poked him in the chest with his forefinger, saying, "Hey! You don't get to talk to me like that!"

"Touch me again, and you'll never talk again, you son of a bitch. Did you do what I asked?"

Dan's bravado faded. He withdrew his hand and put it in his pocket. "Yeah, yeah, it's done. He put up a fight, but I knocked his ass out. By the time he came to, I had both of them hogtied and loaded in the van."

"Are they secured in the galley?"

"Yeah, just like you wanted. I gotta tell you, though, man, I'm never gonna be able to forget the look on their faces. I'm done doing this kind of shit for you. I don't give a rat's ass about the debt I owe you. We're even, man."

"You really think you get to decide when we're even, Dan? Really? I'll tell you when we're even, but don't you worry. It won't be long before your debt will be paid." He laughed as the stun gun brought Dan to the ground. "Not long at all."

He dragged his still-twitching body into the dining room, seating him across from Sandra. Though he kept several pairs of handcuffs nearby, he used Dan's set to secure his feet to the iron grate located in the floor beneath the table. He thought Dan would appreciate the irony of that. His laughter swelled when Dan and Sandra both became conscious of their circumstances at the same time.

"Now that's what I call good timing, you two! Dan, my lovely Sandra has been playing a fun little game all day, but it's just so boring with only one player. That's why you're here. Thank you, by the way, for taking care of that little job for me. Now it's time to finish paying off that debt we were just discussing. Sandra, would you like to explain to Dan how we play this game, or should I?"

His laughter could almost be heard over the noise of the music as he watched Dan's reaction to Sandra's still living, but horribly mutilated body. He didn't even mind the mess that Dan was making. In fact, the vomit and urine would serve nicely as props in the game of choices that Dan would soon be making.

Chapter 58

"Why do I get the feeling that your questions have suddenly taken a personal turn, Nick? Are you perhaps concerned that you might have inherited your father's insanity?" Elise smiled the way a victor might smile at the person she'd just beaten in a race. "Yes, dear Nick, I do indeed know who you are. They do let us keep up with the outside world on occasion. Your father was very special to me, so of course, I kept up with him after he was torn from me."

Nick wasn't sure why he was surprised by this revelation, but he hadn't considered that she might know who he was. He'd played poker with his Uncle Perry and the local boys enough times over the years to have developed a strong poker face. It had always proved useful in interrogations, but he was rarely this caught off guard. His uncle had taught him that the key to covering up surprise was to deflect attention away from your face, giving you enough time to regain composure. Nick instinctively used that knowledge now. He swept his hand across the table, flinging his coffee cup across the room. Elise's eyes followed the cup as it slammed into the wall beside her, then closed tight when the coffee splashed onto her face. By the time she looked back at Nick, he was fully in control of his emotions.

His slanted smile mocked her. "You are partially right, Elise, but only in that my questions are definitely personal. They have nothing to do with my own personal life, however. No, Elise, my questions are all about you and your life. You and your family. I'm curious to know if you were the only psycho bitch from hell in your family, or were your evil genes spread around. Tell me Elise. Is your sister crazy too?"

"You obviously know nothing about my family if you think my inane, prudish sister is anything at all like me. The only smart thing she ever did was leave the country before our game was finished. And since you failed to even mention my brother, I'll fill you in on him as well. He might have had a chance to have some shred of intelligence if the war hadn't destroyed both his body and his mind. We'll never know how he might have turned out."

Traces of spit flew from her mouth as he spoke. Nick knew he couldn't let up now. He had to keep her from hiding behind her poised shell again.

"Sounds to me like you wish you were as smart as your sister, and you're probably thrilled that your brother's superior intelligence was destroyed. But hey, I can understand wanting to be better and smarter than your siblings. Sure, I get it. Did your Daddy think you were the stupid one? Did you have to prove your worth to him?"

He knew he'd struck a nerve. Tears threatened to spill from her eyes, but she held them back.

"I bet your son was smarter than you too, wasn't he? I bet he beat you at your own game as well."

Whatever emotions she might have held in check a moment ago disappeared in a flash. Elise's laughter bounced around the room. "Now I know you're joking! My son? Beat me? He was such a disappointment. I tried everything! Nothing got through to that child. Now your father—oh now, Glen—he should have been my child! He had balls, that one did, and Nick, I can see that you do as well. Don't get me wrong; I had to help Glen find his balls, but of course, that was my pleasure." She paused and ran her tongue across her lips, smiling slyly at Nick.

"Oh yes, Nick, I spent quite a lot of time teaching your father how to make use of his 'gifts'. He was such a troubled young boy, so confused, but ultimately so willing to please me. He was a quick study, easily learning the nuances of gameplay. He understood how choices played a major role in our lives, and what the consequences were of making the wrong choices. But that worthless, dickless bastard of mine could never grasp the enormity of what I was trying to teach him. He was obviously never going to be the man your father would be. I even demonstrated Glen's prowess to him again and again, via the hidden camera installed in each patient's room, but Etienne was never able to measure up. Worthless child. He left the day he was eighteen, and I've not seen him since. Nor do I ever care to lay eyes on that gutless little cur."

Nick went in for the kill. "Oh, but Elise, I think you've underestimated your spawn. As it turns out, he may have out-played, out-maneuvered, and out-witted you by becoming the ultimate master of the evil games you started. And yet here you are, rotting in prison, while he remains free to play his manipulative, destructive games. Right now, he's laughing knowing you ultimately made the wrong choice."

Nick waited until the guards came in to subdue the woman who was screaming incoherently. He'd gotten what he'd come for. He felt certain Etienne was the man behind the murders of the Broussard family, and the person who now threatened Raya and her parents. Now all Nick needed to do was find him.

The evening was turning to night by the time Nick drove back through the prison gates. Once he'd cleared the cellular dead zone, he checked his phone messages. By the time he'd listened to the last one, he was driving 120 mph, his lights flashing; his sirens piercing the night.

Chapter 59

Dustin arrived at George's at 6:45. There was no way he was going to be late for this. He intended to be the first person Sharon noticed when she drove into the parking lot. To accomplish that, he stood directly under the lighted ceiling fan that hung from the porch roof of the old building, giving the appearance of an actor on stage, captured in the spotlight. George's had once been the home of one of Louisiana's most eccentric Cajun novelists, and it still maintained the front façade of its humble beginnings. Over time, it had been expanded—adding an extra 12,000 square feet to the back of the structure—and extensively remodeled on the inside. The front's rustic cedar panels and worn porch was kept intact as a reminder of its rich history. Dustin just hoped it would serve as an appropriate backdrop for him as he leaned casually against one of the columns in his faded jeans and scuffed Justin boots. This might be the best chance he had to break back into Sharon's life after he'd made such a mess of things eighteen months ago.

Raya had called him twenty minutes earlier, so he was not surprised to see Doc's car pull into the lot. He'd hoped to be able to prepare Sharon for the last-minute additions to their meeting, but he'd just have to wing it. When Raya and Jon approached, he shook Jon's hand and gave Raya a hug. "Jon, I have a table reserved in the far back. Just tell the hostess you're with me, and she'll take you two there. I'll join you once my ... once Sharon arrives."

Raya raised her brows. "Sharon?" She let the question hang in the air.

"Sharon is an old ... friend and colleague. I'm hoping she can help us track down our prime suspect. She may be able to help us in various ways, so do me a favor and be nice to her, okay?"

Raya knew that look and suspected there was more to Dustin's relationship with Sharon than he admitted. He looked like a man pleading for his life. "Don't worry, Dustin. We'll be extra nice." Flashing a knowing look at him, she wrapped her arm in Jon's and whisked him into the restaurant.

Dustin resumed his 'casual stance' against the porch post, trying to avoid obsessively checking his watch. At 7:02, beads of sweat began to form on his brow, which he could certainly pass off on the hot, humid evening, but he knew nerves were the real cause. No one but Sharon had ever made Dustin nervous. Guess nothing really changes, he thought. At 7:04, he shifted position, and leaned on the other side of the post. Headlights lit up the lot, blinding him for a moment. When the spots stopped dancing in front of his eyes, he saw her walking towards him. She was as feisty as ever, feet moving in quick short strides, green eyes blazing with intensity. He'd expected steamy anger, but her expression was one of determination rather than rage; as though she was prepared to fight off temptation. If he was right, then that meant temptation still existed, and as long as it did, there was hope.

"Sharon, thank you for allowing me to meet you here. You look amazing." Dustin's smile was genuine.

"Thank you, Dustin. Shall we go inside?" Her polite but cool reply could have been directed at any stranger on the street.

Dustin reached out his hand to stop her progress. "Before we do, Sharon, there's something you should know." He tried to ignore her body language that told him she was wary of whatever he was about to say. "The case has gone from bad to worse rather quickly. Two of the three people that our suspect has targeted have gone missing, and their daughter, the third target is in real danger. I had her pick up a trusted family friend and directed them to meet us here. I didn't mean to spring any of this on you, but everything just happened all of a sudden, after I'd spoken with you. Nick has been unreachable, his uncle Perry has also disappeared, so I figured the only thing I could do was get her here safely and figure out what to do once we were all together."

Sharon placed two fingers on his lips. "Hush. You're rambling, Dustin. I understand. People are in danger, and you did what you needed to do. It's okay. We'll figure this out. Together."

Before he could react, she'd turned and walked into George's and he followed, unsure if everything had just gone as well as it seemed or not.

Chapter 60

"Mom, look, here it is. Come see!" Sue waited for Minnie to put on her reading glasses.

"So, this is what a blog post looks like?" Minnie asked. "Looks just like a plain old news story to me."

"It's really not much different than that, Mom. It doesn't matter anyway. Let's see what Raya has to say about the case." The two women, Sue seated at her desk, and Minnie bent over her daughter's shoulder, read the post silently to themselves.

Bayou Family Slaughter Case – Master Gamesman Outwits Law For Two Decades

For more than two decades, a killer has eluded police in what can only be described as a perfect show of gamesmanship. Glen Simoneaux, who was once a patient of another mistress of evil, is the prime suspect in a gruesome murder that took place twenty years ago.

The story begins with a female psychiatrist named Elise Beraud who was the head of a mental institution in Mississippi thirty years ago. For years before that, she'd run cruel and illegal experiments on the patients under her care. These experiments were designed to test her theory that she had the power—as a gamemaster—to not only predict what choices humans would make, given a prescribed set of shocking selections to choose from, but she could even force them to unknowingly make the choice she preferred. The games she played often involved physical mutilation, sexual degradation, or mental torture. She was eventually arrested and convicted and is now serving a life sentence. The mental institution was promptly shut down.

Glen Simoneaux, her favorite patient and prodigy, was released at that time, and a decade later, he became the leading suspect in the murder of a prominent family in the small town of St. Felicity, Louisiana. The murders of Randy Broussard, his wife, and their two young children have been described as brutal and horrific, but the details of the crime scene made it clear that Elise Beraud's cruel games had just been recreated with even more depravity than she'd ever imagined.

Dr. Beraud's favorite experimental patient had eclipsed her in the mastery of her own game. While she has been rotting in prison, Glen has eluded the law for the last twenty years, proving that he is the master of the game now.

Next week's post will highlight the clever skill and mastery of gameplay that Mr. Simoneaux used in both the Broussard case and in his ability to resist capture. Until he is caught, watch your back. You may be the target of his next devious game.

Minnie tapped the screen with her finger. "Why did Raya say that about Glen? I don't understand! Did she uncover information that we didn't know about? I mean, sure, Glen was a possible suspect, but she's making it sound like there's no doubt about it at all!"

"I don't know, Momma," Sue said. "If she found new evidence, she didn't tell me about it. Oh, this will break poor Nick's heart."

"Not to mention what dear Margaret must be thinking right now. I should call on her; make sure she's okay, don't you think, Sue?"

"I guess so, Momma. You do that, and I'll make a few calls around town to see if I can find out where Raya got the idea that Glen was definitely the killer. Keep your phone on, Momma. I'll call you if I find out anything. Give Ms. Margaret a hug for me and tell her not to worry. We'll stand beside her, no matter what her husband did."

Chapter 61

Thirty minutes later, he was regretting that his time with her was done. Sandra had finally forfeited the game; her lifeless body slumped over the table. Dan was currently passed out, so he decided to check his messages while he waited for the game to resume. Five texts and three voicemails cried out for attention; each just a variation of the others. That blogger had named Glen Simoneaux as the killer and was calling him a clever master of gameplay. Two of the texts gave the web address of the blog post. The game would have to wait. He needed to see for himself what the bitch had written.

He sat in the guest room, which he used as his home office on occasion, with the iPad on his lap. He'd read the blog post three times by now, and his rage was no longer controllable. His plan to make her wait for days before leading her to the boat, where she would find her bloodied, tortured parents would have to be changed. He needed to play the game now. No more practice rounds.

He removed the machete from the old wooden case. He'd not used it in twenty years, but he'd sharpened the blade every year on the anniversary of the Broussard murders. He ran the blade across his thigh, slicing it open in one clean motion. The blood stain grew, soaking his pants leg, inciting his rage. He walked to the dining room. Dan was still passed out, his forehead resting on the table. He grasped Dan's hair in his free hand, just as he'd done with Sandra earlier in the day. The feel of the hair between his fingers caused his erection to grow, just like it had with Sandra. He brought Dan's head backwards until his face pointed up toward the ceiling. With a loud scream, he brought the machete up and then down with brutal force. The first time sliced through most of Dan's neck, but he continued hacking until it came free of the body it was once attached to. He held the head high, in the manner of a winner raising his trophy, and released his seed at last. Yes, he was the master of the game. She would find that out soon enough.

Since access to the boat would require going out in public, he showered and changed clothes, then filled a duffle bag with several items that would be needed for maximum game enjoyment. He didn't bother to hide evidence or clean the crime scene. He left the house exactly as it was, knowing he would never return. This time, no one would wonder who the gamemaster might be. His name would become legend. He picked up the final items he would need: his cell phone, the iPad, and another red, three-sided dice.

"It is time you learn my name, Raya Landry."

Chapter 62

Raya allowed Dustin to introduce Sharon before she interrupted. "If you don't mind, can we skip the pleasantries for now? My parents are missing and frankly, I don't want to waste time discussing anything other than a plan to find them."

Sharon said, "Point taken, Raya. I agree. Let's get right down to business. Can you quickly bring me up to speed on the details? Why do you believe they are missing? When did you discover them missing? When was the last time anyone has had contact with them?"

Raya summarized her search and findings up to this point. "As far as I know, the last time anyone saw them was when we all left their house at two a.m. this morning."

Jon added, "And on the way here, I called everyone I could think of that might have seen them today. No one has."

Sharon typed a note into her smart phone. "That means we can't officially report them as missing until tomorrow morning, since they must be missing at least 24 hours before a report can be filed with the local authorities. If we haven't found your parents by then, Raya, you and I will notify the Lafayette police together."

"Sharon, if we knew where our suspect lives, we might be able to determine where he might be keeping Dennis and Janet," Dustin said. He turned to Raya and said, "What you don't know yet is that I've narrowed down our list of suspects to one person— Etienne Beraud. He is the son of the former Dr. Elise Beraud who was the head of a psychiatric institution in Mississippi until she was arrested and charged with various crimes, all involving illegal and unethical experiments on patients under her care. DNA evidence revealed that someone who is very closely related to her is our killer. For various reasons, only her son, Etienne, could possibly be the one who killed the Broussards and the one who is targeting you and your parents.

Unfortunately, there has been no trace of Etienne since he left home a decade before he killed the Broussard family. I asked Sharon to meet me tonight because she is from the same area where Etienne grew up, and she has many law enforcement contacts in the entire deep south region. I'm hoping she can help us find Mr. Beraud." Looking at Sharon, he continued, "Sharon? Is there any chance you know Etienne or have any information on his current whereabouts?"

Of course, the history of that institution and Dr. Beraud's experiments are well known to me. I was a newborn when that took place, so I don't actually remember any of it, but it's a large part of my hometown's history. I'm sorry to say that I don't know Etienne or where he might be, but I do have a lot of contacts who may know him or who may have a record of his movements and activities over the years. I'll start contacting them the moment we finish our conversation here."

"We may not have to wait for someone to tell us where he is," Raya said.

Both Dustin and Sharon looked at Raya with surprise. "Why do say that?" Dustin asked.

"As you know, Dustin, part of the plan we devised last night was for me to lay down some bait for our suspect. We decided I would publish blog posts about the Broussard case that would likely push the killer out of hiding. This morning, Nick suspected Dr. Beraud had some information that might be of use, so asked me to hold off on publishing the post until he'd interrogated her. However, since no one has heard from Nick, and my parents' lives are at stake, I published the post about an hour ago. I then made sure word spread throughout St. Felicity. With any luck, Etienne will read the post and become angry enough to reach out to me. I only hope he doesn't take his anger out on Mom and Dad." She could not hold back the tears any longer. Jon pulled her close and let her cry in his arms.

Sharon opened the Chrome browser on her smart phone and asked Raya for the URL of the blog post. After she, Dustin, and Jon read it, she said, "I think your plan just may work, if Etienne reads the post, and if his ego overrides his caution. However, we can't rely on that happening, so let's continue searching for him in the meantime. We also need to try to contact Nick and Perry, since they may be missing as well. If they are reachable, then we need to coordinate our next steps with them as soon as possible."

Dustin took a deep breath before plunging in. "I'll work on contacting Nick and Perry. In the meantime, Raya's safety is a priority. I was wondering, Sharon, if you would mind letting Jon and Raya stay in your room tonight? I…"

Sharon interrupted. "No explanation needed, Dustin. I'm staying in a fairly large suite, so there's plenty of room, and yes, I think that's a good idea." Looking directly at Raya, she continued. "You'll be safe with me, Raya. We can discuss my credentials later, if you'd like, but for now, I hope you'll just trust us on this point."

Raya nodded. "I have no reason to distrust either of you. I don't know where else to go anyway. If Doc doesn't mind, we'd be grateful to share your suite with you."

Jon agreed, and the four decided to get started right away. Dustin pulled Sharon aside. "Sharon, I can't thank you enough for this."

Sharon smiled and reached for his hands. "Dustin, I may kick myself later, but for now, let's just move forward and start fresh. Just don't give me a reason to regret this decision."

"I won't, I promise," Dustin assured her.

"Good. Then go home now. Do your best to find Nick and Perry. Call me as soon as you have any information to share, and I'll do the same. Even if neither of us has new info, let's talk again at eleven p.m. tonight. I'll call you at that time."

An unspoken understanding passed between them as they left. Dustin watched as Jon and Raya followed Sharon's car. He waited until they were out of sight before leaving the lot. He then drove home, his mind and heart whirling with mixed emotions. Worry for his friends and hope for a rekindled relationship with Sharon disrupted his normally carefree disposition. Emotions. Worry. Caring. Maybe this is what I've been missing in my life, he thought. That thought only succeeded in adding a touch of fear to the assortment of emotions running through him.

Chapter 63

Sharon's hotel suite was designed not for luxury or romance, but for business use, which equally suited all three occupants. The sleeping area contained two queen size beds, two small corner desks, one wall-mounted TV and two separate closets. A small balcony was accessible via sliding glass doors on the far side of the bedroom. The business work room consisted of a large desk (fully equipped with phone, printer, scanner, and fax), a full-size sofa bed, a small flat-screen television, and a wet bar. The suite also came with a fully-stocked kitchenette and wireless Internet access was available throughout the suite.

It was quickly decided that Sharon and Raya would each choose one of the queen beds in the bedroom, and Jon would sleep on the sofa bed in the work room. Jon sat at the work room desk, opened the center drawer, and withdrew the standard hotel-branded notepad and ink pen. He decided to make a few more discreet calls to people who might have seen Dennis and Janet earlier in the day, and he wanted to be able to jot down notes if necessary. Sharon paced the bedroom, speaking to seemingly no one. Raya finally realized that Sharon had a Bluetooth ear piece hiding under her mass of auburn curls, enabling her to speak hands-free via her cell phone, which was lying on her bed.

Needing time alone, Raya stepped out onto the balcony, making sure the curtains stayed closed as she slipped through the sliding glass doors. At any other time, she would have appreciated the expansive view of the city lights. Tonight, however, they only served to highlight how difficult it would be to find two people across a huge expanse of territory. Desperate, she decided to speak to the darkness, in hopes her words might somehow travel across the wavelengths that separated her from her parents.

"Mom, Dad, I know you're out there somewhere, scared, and maybe even hurt. Stay strong and have faith that we'll find you! This is all my fault. If I hadn't gone to St. Felicity, you wouldn't be missing right now. I promise I'll do everything in my power to find you and rescue you. I just need you to do everything you can to stay alive and well until I reach you. Don't give up! Please, don't give up."

Before her was the state's capitol, Baton Rouge. To the left, farther than she could see, lay the city of Lafayette, where she'd last seen her parents. To the right, again out of sight, lay the small town of St. Felicity, where she believed they might be at this moment.

"Etienne may have taken you anywhere," she said, "but I think he's hidden you somewhere in St. Felicity. You know, Mom and Dad, that I'm no psychiatrist, but I've written about a lot of killers over the years. The one trait they all tend to share is their need for maintaining control. One of the ways they accomplish that is to stay within their comfort zones. I'd bet that Etienne imagines himself to be a master manipulator and the puppet master over the victims of his own twisted games. To control those games, he'll need to play them in familiar surroundings, where he can assume there won't be any unexpected surprises. So, unless I hear something to make me change my mind, I'm going to start searching for you in St. Felicity. Hopefully, you'll find a way to let me feel your presence there."

Raya's cell phone buzzed, vibrating from her jeans pocket. She quickly pulled it out and looked at the number displayed on the screen, but she didn't recognize it. "Hello?"

"Your parents are safe and waiting for you to join them. Come alone to the old Broussard estate in St. Felicity. If you aren't alone, your parents will die slowly and painfully." The voice was spoken in a half whisper / half grunt, obviously intended to mask the caller's real voice.

"Please, don't hurt them! I'll do anything you ask!" Raya begged.

"Shut up and listen. The game begins in half an hour. Every half hour, a new round of play will take place. The longer it takes you to arrive, the more rounds your parents will have to play. It is entirely up to you how much they will have to endure while they wait for you to join the game, Raya. I wish you could be here for the first roll of the dice. The beginning of the game is always so exhilarating."

The phone clicked and to Raya's horror, the display showed Call Ended. "No! Dammit!" Raya quickly calculated the time it would take to get to the Broussard estate in St. Felicity from the hotel in Baton Rouge. She assumed it would be at least an hour, but if she left right away and drove fast enough, she might be able to cut the time down to forty-five minutes. She couldn't possibly make it within half an hour, so she wouldn't be able to prevent the first roll of the dice, but if she hurried, she might be able to prevent it from rolling a second time.

I have to get out of here unnoticed, she thought. And on top of that, I have to somehow steal Doc's or Sharon's keys because I don't have my own car here. Dammit! I can do this. I have to do this!

Raya took three long deep breaths, forced her facial muscles to relax, and then walked back into the suite. Sharon was still pacing and only glanced at Raya before concentrating again on the floor in front of her feet while she spoke through her headset. Raya casually glanced around but didn't see Sharon's keys anywhere. She then strolled into the work room. Doc was still seated at the desk, his back towards her. He was holding his phone to his ear, nodding his head and grunting in affirmation. He was completely unaware of her presence in the room. Her eyes scanned the sofa and end tables, and then moved to the floor where his briefcase rested. There, on top of the case was a set of keys. She recognized them immediately. Looking back over her shoulder, she waited until Sharon's pacing took her out of view, and then carefully swept the keys up into her palm, trying to rattle them as little as possible. The slight tinkling noise they made didn't reach Doc's ears, so she quickly slipped out of the suite, closing the door behind her as silently as possible.

She ran down the hall until she reached the intersecting hallway which led to the elevators. Looking back one last time to make sure no one was chasing after her, she turned the corner, ran to the elevator and pushed the button several times, rapidly. "Come on, come on!" she whispered. Eight seconds later, the elevator doors opened. By the time Doc and Sharon noticed she was gone, Raya was several miles down the highway, racing towards St. Felicity.

Twenty minutes later, Raya pulled off the highway, onto the shoulder and parked. She composed a text message that read, *"Killer called. Told me to meet him and my parents at Broussard estate – alone. Had to give myself a head start. Sorry."* She decided that would give enough information to ensure she would have backup eventually. She just needed a little time to convince the bastard that she had come alone – as instructed, but she was smart enough to know she would eventually need help. Satisfied with the message, she sent it to Doc's phone, and then pulled back onto the highway, quickly accelerating to 95 mph. She knew she'd never make it to the estate before the game began, but she was determined to get there before her parents had to make a second choice.

Forty-eight minutes had passed when Raya pulled into the long driveway. Stepping out of the car, she looked around, seeing no one. Come on, you bastard, I'm here! Where are you? she thought. Taking a few steps towards the house, she heard her cell ring inside the car. "Shit!" She fumbled with the door handle, flung open the door and dived in to reach the phone. "Hello!"

"Such a shame that you didn't get here earlier, Raya. It would have been such fun to see your reaction as your father carved the word 'slut' into your mother's back. Of course, I had hoped he would make no choice, because that would have allowed me to carve it on her face, but the game is far from over, so I'll get my turn soon."

"Where are you? Come out of hiding you little coward. Come get me you son of a bitch!" Raya again stepped out of the car, phone to her ear, searching the grounds for any sign of life.

"Oh, don't worry, Raya. I'm right here. You and I will return to the place where your parents are waiting, and you'll get to watch as someone takes his or her last breath. Who do you think it will be, Raya? Your father? Your mother? Or you? Time to find out!" Raya detected the pungent smell, sensing what it was, but she didn't have time to duck away from the hand that reached over her shoulder; she didn't have time to avoid the cloth that was pressed tightly over her face.

Chapter 64

Nick cursed Perry for not answering his phone again. "Dammit, man, I left you in charge of Raya. Where the hell are you!" Next, he tried Dustin's number, but was sent to voice mail immediately, which usually meant Dustin was on another call. Nick assumed he could reach Dustin soon, but in the meantime, he tried phoning Dennis, Jon, and of course Raya. Each call ended in frustration. Even Dan didn't answer. "What the hell?"

As Nick neared St. Felicity, he reached for the phone again, but just as he flipped it open, it rang.

"Hello? Dustin! What the hell is going on?" Nick didn't realize he was shouting.

"Things have quickly gone from bad to worse here, Nick. Where are you, and how soon will you be back?"

"I'm not far from St. Felicity now. I'll probably be there in ten minutes or so. Should I head there, or keep going to Baton Rouge to meet you, or drive all the way to Lafayette? Tell me where I should go!"

"Go straight to the Broussard estate in St. Felicity, Nick. Jon and Sharon and I are all headed there now."

"Sharon? As in your Sharon?" Nick asked.

"Yeah, man, she's helping out. I'll explain later. Anyway, I'd arranged for Raya and Jon to stay with Sharon tonight, but apparently Raya got a call to meet Etienne alone at the Broussard estate. He claims he has her parents there. She snuck out so she could follow his demands and meet him there alone, but luckily, she sent a text message to Jon a little later, letting him know where she was headed. So, we're all converging there. We're about fifteen minutes away at this point, so we should be getting there at nearly the same time as you."

"Son of a bitch! What was she thinking?!" Nick slammed his hand against the steering wheel, causing the car to slide a little. That jolted him back to reality. He knew he couldn't help Raya if he spun out of control at 120 mph.

Dustin ignored that question and continued summing up the situation for Nick. "So far, we still don't know what happened to Perry, but…"

"Wait a minute, we'll get to Perry in a minute. I just realized you mentioned Etienne. That's Elise's son. So, you know for sure he's the one?"

"It can't be anyone else, Nick. I'm as sure as I can be at this point," Dustin replied.

"Okay, good. I came to the same conclusion after interviewing Elise today, but I'm glad to hear it confirmed. Do we know anything else about this guy yet?"

"No, sorry, Sharon was in the process of tracking down leads on that when we realized Raya was gone."

Nick's phone chirped, indicating a second call was coming through. He glanced at the screen and saw Perry's name there. "Dustin, Perry's calling in. Let me take that. I'll see you in a few." Nick didn't wait for Dustin's reply. He hung up and answered Perry's call.

"Perry! Are you okay? Where are you? What happened to you?" Again, Nick was shouting without realizing it.

"Nick, it's been the day from hell. I was following Raya to her parents' home when I had a blowout. I tried to call her; hell, I tried to call everyone, but I've been having trouble with my damn phone for days now. I couldn't get through to anyone. It's taken me this long to get back on the road and to finally get a call out. Tell Raya I'm really sorry…"

"I can't tell Raya anything! She's meeting the killer right now! Alone! I depended on you to watch over her, Perry!"

"What?! Damn, Nick, do we know where she's meeting that son of a bitch?" Already, Perry's foot was pressing the car's pedal to the floor. He didn't know where he was going yet, but he was damn sure planning to get there fast.

"She sent a text to Jon saying she was meeting Etienne Beraud at the old Broussard estate. Apparently, he already has her parents there. They've been missing most of the day."

"Etienne Beraud? Is he related to the Dr. Beraud who ran the institution?" Perry asked.

"Yeah, he's her son. We'll get the details later, but for now, we believe he's our guy. I'm just getting to St. Felicity now, I should be at the estate in two minutes. Meet me there!" Nick ended the call and turned off his siren. He didn't want to announce his arrival to Etienne just yet.

Chapter 65

Nick noticed the gate to the estate was open, but he didn't want to drive up the driveway, so he continued driving, and then parked on the side of the road about 500 yards away. He walked back up the road, and upon entering the gate, he quickly ducked behind the dense, seven-foot tall Ligustrum bushes that surrounded the property. There was a gap of about two feet between the hedges and the fence, allowing him to stay hidden as he worked his way towards the side entrance of the estate. He was grateful he didn't have allergies, as the shrubs were in full bloom, and while the smell was sweet and intoxicating, it was a major allergy trigger for many people who lived in the area. He was depending upon stealth. A burst of sneezing would ruin that plan.

Once he reached the area just opposite the side entrance, he could see the driveway's end, and parked there was Jon's vehicle, in much the same place as it had been when they'd all met here just two days ago. It was the only car here this time, however, and there was no evidence of anyone around. He listened closely but could hear nothing but the hundreds of crickets and frogs that sang in the night. He decided the darkness would keep his presence a secret, as long as he crossed the yard quickly. He couldn't help the fact that the crickets and frogs went silent as he ran to the door, but he considered it lucky that they resumed their songs only seconds later.

Even in the darkness, he could tell that the door still retained a decades-old doorknob and lock, so he was able to gain entry with a swipe of an old credit card. He waited until his eyes adjusted to the even darker interior of the house before moving forward. He didn't want to trip over anything. Stealth was even more important now.

He worked his way through the kitchen, finding his way to the adjoining dining room and living room where the original crime had taken place. He saw and heard nothing to indicate that anyone was here. He made his way up the stairs, wincing when the steps creaked. As quickly as he could, while maintaining silence, he made his way through every room of the house but found nothing.

Making his way back downstairs, he double-checked the rooms on the ground floor, and when he was satisfied that the house was empty, he left through the front door. Standing on the porch, he surveyed the surroundings. Nothing stood out that would indicate where four people might be hiding. Most of the estate's grounds consisted open lawn, with no unattached buildings.

Suddenly, an unfamiliar car roared into view, screaming up the driveway. Nick ducked behind the porch swing and aimed his gun at the doors that were opening. The car's interior light illuminated Dustin's face, and Nick recognized Jon and Sharon next. Since anyone here would now know they weren't alone, Nick decided calling out was not only acceptable but probably wise. "Dustin! Nick here—on the porch."

"Nick! That's my car!" shouted Jon.

Nick strode toward the group. "I know. I've checked the entire house. There's no one here."

Sharon said, "It's possible he met her here, and then took her somewhere else. That would ensure his ultimate location remained hidden."

"She had a twenty minute head start on us," Dustin said. "They could be pretty far away by now." Nick shook his head. "They could be, yes, but I don't think so. He's here, in the area, somewhere. I don't know where, but I'd bet he's got them stashed somewhere nearby. It would help if we had any information on this guy."

Sharon nodded, saying, "Yes it would, but right now all we have is the evidence at hand. Nick, you and I should inspect Jon's car. Maybe Raya left a clue there. Dustin, you take Jon with you and go through the house one more time. It's possible Nick missed something. We'll meet back here and cover the grounds together."

Ten minutes later, when they gathered again, Nick said, "Time is speeding by, and we've found nothing. Dammit! Raya, where are you!"

Dustin and Jon looked to Sharon for guidance but for now she was out of answers. "Let's go over everything we know one more time," she suggested.

"Better yet, why don't we try to find the answers to what we don't know yet," replied Nick. "Dustin said you were in the process of finding out more about Etienne. Why don't you get back on that task, Sharon? Wait, my phone is buzzing!" Nick answered, saying only, "What? We'll be right there."

He hung up and looked at the three faces staring back at him. With a catch in his voice, he said, "That was Perry. He just heard from one of the men on the force. There's a report of a double homicide over at Sandra Hebert's place."

No one said a word. They simply jumped into Sharon's car and quickly sped away.

Chapter 66

Perry was waiting out front, speaking to Henshaw, when they arrived at the scene. Nick jumped from the car before Sharon had rolled to a stop. "Perry, is it…?" Nick's eyes pleaded with Perry for good news.

"No, Nick, it's not Raya or her parents," Perry said.

Nick's relief was evident but was soon replaced by worry that they had been called out on a wild goose chase and may have lost valuable time in their search. "Who is it then, Perry?"

Henshaw interrupted. "I found 'em, Nick. It's pretty bad in there. One of 'em is Miss Sandra. And the other one, well, it was Officer Dan."

"Dan? Dan Guidry is dead? And Sandra too? How? What happened? Never mind, I'll go see for myself."

Perry reached out to stop him. "Nick, be prepared."

"Yeah, I get it. It's bad. Sharon, come with me. Dustin stay out here with Jon. Perry, find out all you can from anyone in the area. And quickly!"

Nick led Sharon through the front door. He only had to follow the blood trail to find the crime scene. Sandra, or what was left of her, sat at the table. The parts missing from her lay neatly arranged on the table in front of her. Opposite Sandra, the headless torso of a man was slumped over the table. Blood spatters decorated the walls, ceiling, table and floor, while thick pools of blood had settled both on and under the table. Several feet away, on the floor near the couch, another pool of blood had collected just under Dan's severed head.

Nick stared at Dan's eyes, unsure if what he was seeing was real or not. Sharon tried to draw his attention away, but Nick brushed her off. "Look," he said. He pointed towards the head.

"Yes, I see it, Nick. I'm sorry. I assume you knew him," Sharon replied.

"No. I mean, yes, I knew Dan. But that's not what I mean. Look. There. In the blood pool."

Sharon saw what he was pointing at now. Lying in the thick dark blood was a small pyramid-shaped object.

"The dice," Nick said.

He ran out, shouting now for Perry and Dustin. "It's him, it's him! The dice! It's in there. He did this!" Nick grabbed Perry by his shoulders. "Did you find out anything from anyone here? What about Ethan? He lives here too, with Sandra! Has anyone seen him or contacted him?"

Perry's eyes widened. "That's it, Nick. That's what we've been missing."

"What?" Nick shouted.

"Ethan. Ethan Breaux. Etienne. Etienne Beraud." Jon said, "Ethan. That makes sense. Ethan wasn't from here. He came to town maybe two or three years before you and your brother showed up, Perry. No one questioned his name. Why would we?"

Sharon said, "We can get into the details later. For now, we need to get moving. Get every available officer on this. I'll call in for help from the surrounding areas. Now that we know who we are looking for, we stand a much better chance of finding him, but we need to get on it!"

As the others started to drift away, Jon said, "Guys? Guys!"

They turned back to him. "What is it, Jon?" Nick asked.

Jon was staring at the phone in his hand. "I just got another text message from Raya. It says 'buried shrimp'. That's all it says."

"Let me see that!" Nick grabbed the phone from Jon. "Buried shrimp? Does that mean anything to anyone here?" Nick yelled, and then yelled again, louder this time. "Buried shrimp! Buried shrimp. Does anyone know what that might mean?"

Henshaw tapped Nick on the back and spoke softly. "Nick? I think I know what it means."

Chapter 67

Raya glared defiantly at Ethan. "No," she said.

"'No' is not a choice, Raya. 'A' is a choice. 'B' is a choice. Even 'X' is a choice, if you've decided to choose neither 'A' nor 'B'. By saying, 'No', are you really choosing 'X'?"

"No," she repeated.

"Fine then, every time you say 'No' to me, I'll assume you really mean 'X'".

"I don't care what you assume, Ethan. I am not playing your stupid petty little game. I'm not afraid of you." Raya stared into his eyes, refusing to look at her parents. He'd forced her to watch as he traced the wounds on her mother's back with his tongue when she'd first arrived, causing her mother to cry out in pain. She wouldn't let him use them further to weaken her resolve.

Ethan slapped her face, then slapped it again just to feel the sting against his palm once more. Dennis struggled against the ropes holding him down, trying to scream through the gag. Janet closed her eyes, tears continuing to stream, despite hours of crying.

"You will play, bitch, or your parents will suffer the consequences."

"Do what you want to them, I don't care!" Raya finally looked at her parents. "They stole my life from me! They are no better than you are! All of you think you can control me, but none of you will ever have control over me again!" Raya leaned back, and then flung herself forward, shooting spit in a high arc that landed directly on her mother's face. "There you go, Mother! Add that to your tears!"

Turning away, Raya focused on Ethan again. "You think you are in control, but you are nothing but a sniveling coward, afraid of your own mommy. Well guess what, Etienne, your mommy hates you. She thinks you're a useless, pitiful excuse for a son. You've never been in control. Your mother has always controlled you—and the game. But not even your mother can control me. This game is my game now. My game!"

"Shut up! Shut the fuck up!" Ethan climbed out of the galley, leaving them alone in the dark.

Raya lowered her voice to less than a whisper. "Mom, Dad, I'm so sorry. You know I didn't mean that. Please, just hang in there with me. We'll make it out of this, I promise!"

The love emanating from the eyes of her parents told her all she needed to know and gave her the strength to finish this on her terms. She'd come more prepared than Ethan might have imagined. Although she was tied to the chair, Ethan had left one hand free to use the dice. She took the dice, placed it in her pocket, and retrieved the dice she had brought with her from the other pocket. She placed it on the table. Raya thought she could see her parents smiling behind the gags, as they stared at the broken, crushed pile of red plastic that lay there.

Ethan soon returned, speaking and smiling as he descended the ladder. "I've decided you don't have to play the game, Raya. Your parents and I will play instead. I'll deal with you later." At the last step, he turned toward Janet, displaying his erection proudly. Pleased with the reaction he received from Janet and Dennis, he pivoted and reached for the dice on the table. Silently, he picked up the shattered remnants of the dice. Raya observed the bulge in his pants disappear in tandem with the pieces of plastic that fell through his fingers.

Enraged, Ethan tried to lift the table, intending to throw it at Raya, but the old bolts that secured it to the deck held fast. Screaming, he scrambled to find anything in the cabin that he could throw. As he reached for a cup he'd left there one day long ago, Dennis was able to move his foot an inch forward; just enough to trip Ethan. Ethan's forehead slammed into a metal hook used to secure line, and his knees buckled under him. Dazed, with blood obscuring his vision, Ethan roared like a wounded bear.

Chapter 68

Nick, Sharon, Perry, and Jon followed Henshaw, running through the scrub brush that grew fast and thick in the woods surrounding the bayous. Despite his age, Henshaw was still in better shape than most men in their twenties. He would hurt later, but at the moment, his speed was not hampered by age.

They'd driven as far as possible, right up to the fence that Henshaw and his boys had built upon Ethan's request. There was no time to look for a boat that might have a key hanging from the ignition, so they ran along the edge of the canal, trying to weave through the thinnest areas of brush. They'd run about a mile, when he saw the old trot line he'd left tied to a cypress tree years ago. He knew they were close then, but he didn't have to tell the others that the shrimp boat was just up ahead. They all heard the screams at the same time.

Adrenaline surged through Nick when he heard the screams, and he burst forward, speeding past Henshaw. Within a tight circle of cypress trees, a few feet from the bank, he could just make out the bow of the boat shimmering through the sweat that dripped in his eyes.

Nick leaped from the bank to the first cypress knee, a unique woody root formation that grows upwards around cypress trees. Holding onto a nearby tree trunk, he jumped to the next knee, and finally leaped towards the boat, his right hand finding a cleat and his left grasping the rope wrapped around it. Using the momentum from his jump, he heaved his body onto the deck. The deck was slick with wet algae, causing him to slide hip first, several feet until a low-hanging branch punched through his thigh, effectively stopping his progress. Pulling his leg free, Nick stood and looked towards the screams. He could hear Dustin and the others climbing aboard the boat from the other side, but he didn't wait for help. Hoping he could keep his footing, he ran full speed into the galley door, bursting through it and falling straight down on top of Ethan's back. Ethan bucked Nick off, sending both of them tumbling across the laps of Dennis and Janet. The chairs collapsed and all four bodies crashed to the deck.

Nick was trapped under one of the chairs, with Ethan laying on top, his back facing Nick. While they all struggled to get upright, Nick reached around the leg of Dennis's chair, and wrapped his arm around Ethan's neck. He pulled Ethan towards him, squeezing as hard as he could, straining to keep Ethan from struggling free. Ethan used his hips to twist and turn his lower body, forcing Nick to lose his grip. Ethan flung his body forward, howling victoriously. He lunged across the table, intending to strangle Raya the way Nick had just tried to strangle him. His fingers stretched across the table, his eyes locked onto her neck. He never saw the plank, but he felt the sudden rush of air just before Henshaw slammed it through his skull.

Chapter 69

Twelve hours later, Nick stood with his arm around Raya, waving goodbye to Dennis and Janet. After being released from the hospital, they were anxious to return home to Lafayette. Their statements had been taken, and their wounds would heal. Dan's wife would live with the knowledge that her husband had been dirty and had died at the hands of the demon he had served. The town was struggling to cope with another tragedy brought on by the same evil that had changed their lives decades before, but this time, a sense of peace was interwoven with the sadness and loss.

Raya turned to Jon. "Thank you for all your help, Doc."

"You were the one who made all the difference, Raya. Your courage in taking control of the game kept Ethan from carrying out whatever plan he had. And I should thank you for giving me the opportunity to fall in love with my home town again."

"So, you really plan to move back here, Doc?"

"As soon as I'm sure that your parents are coping with all of the trauma they've been through, I'll put my current practice on the market and move back here. What about you, Raya? Have you decided what you'll do now?"

Raya felt Nick's arm tense. She smiled up at him and said, "Whatever I want to do. I'm in control of my life now. I need to finish writing this blog series and clear Glen's name. After that, I'm not sure. It's too soon to decide everything. I do plan to keep the name I've used for the last twenty years. I think Raya suits me. But I don't know if I'll stay in Lafayette or not. Luckily, my career choice doesn't decide that for me. I can do my job as a 'grave blogger' from anywhere in the world. I have a feeling, though, that I'll be seeing you again, Nick. At least, I hope so!"

Nick's arm relaxed. Smiling down at Raya, Nick said, "You can count on it, chér."

###

About the author

Donna Fontenot Cavalier, née Donna D. Fontenot, is a native of Baton Rouge, Louisiana, and grew up in a typical Cajun family that focused on good food and good fun (which usually involved either LSU football or fishing and other water-related activities). The Grave Blogger, her first novel, was born from her love of a good mystery and her fascination with the twisted mechanisms of criminal minds. Using her own experience as a blogger, she brought all of her interests and life experiences together into a fascinating tale of mystery and suspense.

Connect with Donna online:

Twitter:
https://twitter.com/DonnaCavalier

Blog:
https://www.donnacavalier.com

The Grave Blogger book website:
https://thegraveblogger.com